# ALL TIED UP IN KNOTZ

*by Andres Cyanni Halden*

# All Tied Up In Knotz

Cover artwork by Soro
http://www.furaffinity.net/user/Soro

**Published by FurPlanet Productions**
Dallas, Texas
www.furplanet.com

Print ISBN 978-1-61450-128-2
ebook ISBN 978-1-61450-129-9

Printed in the United States of America
First Edition Trade Paperback 2013
Electronic Edition 2013

Other books by Andres Cyanni Halden:


Within Hallowed Walls
A Single Quavering Note
Beyond Hallowed Walls
Transcending Hallowed Walls
Seeing Spots


The Fortune Teller's Poem (editor)
Holidays (editor)


Order at FurPlanet.com or scan the code below:

# Table of Contents

# Chapter One: Carpe Vulpes

Carson looked up at the sky, trying to get his eyes to re-focus. The fox was on his back, his bike strewn on the road a few yards from him. Pain radiated down one arm, though his legs felt fine. He sat up, realized a bit too late that was a bad decision, and immediately leaned to the side, very nauseous. A paw touched his back, and he jerked away, wiping his mouth to see if he'd busted his lip. That had also been a bad decision, since his paw was covered in gravel.

"Are you alright?" someone asked. Looking around, he saw what was left of his phone in a pile of leaky glass. Dammit. His hookup app, Knotz, was stuck on the screen. Looking further around, there was a black bear standing behind him, and the car that had hit him had the driver's door open.

"I did not see you, I am so sorry," the bear said. Carson looked up, still woozy. The bear wore a green tracksuit and had an accent the fox couldn't place at the moment. When the fox looked back down, he realized his work clothes were pretty much ruined.

"I need to call…" He swallowed another wave of nausea. "…never mind."

"I will take you to hospital," the bear said and reached down to try and pick him up. Carson waved his good arm.

"No insurance," he said. "I need to go home." Horns honked, and a couple of people leaned out of car windows to yell at both of them.

"I will take you."

Carson looked over at his bike. The frame was bent. How much would that cost to fix? He had some savings, but he wasn't looking forward to paying for a new bike.

"Fine," he whispered, and took the offered paw.

"I am Peter."

The bear helped him into the passenger seat and then took off his jacket, carefully tying it around the fox's bloody arm. He had a wife-beater on underneath it. The inside of his car smelled like tobacco, but more like the plant than cigarettes. When the bear popped open the glove box, the fox noticed a small box of cigars, and the bear handed him a bottle of aspirin and a small, open bottle of water from the cup holder. Well, the fox couldn't be picky right now. He quickly took two. The bear then picked up the fox's ruined bike, threw it in the trunk, and came back around into the car.

"Turn left," Carson said after he swallowed.

The fox didn't know cars, but he did know this was an expensive one. The seats were insanely comfortable, all of the paneling looked like real wood, and he barely felt it when they went over a pothole. He kept giving directions as they drove a few blocks, while Peter kept looking over at him. It took the fox a few minutes to realize that the bear probably didn't speak English as a first language and might be reading his lips.

"It's right here," Carson said. The fox pointed to a tall apartment building, forlornly standing between two larger, newer buildings. There wasn't any parking in front of the building, so the fox had expected the bear to stop and just let him out, but he instead drove a block down into the closest parking garage.

Peter parked the car, got out, walked around, and opened the passenger door for him. What else was going on here? His mind didn't immediately go to sex, but when the bear put an arm around his waist to help him steady when he stepped out, his sheath definitely went there. He hadn't noticed it so much in the car, but the bear had a thick, almost overpowering musk. He didn't smell dirty, just very masculine. Carson swallowed, trying to figure out how he could be in pain, slightly nauseated, and still attracted to someone at the same time.

They walked to the elevator out of the parking lot, took it down, and walked the short distance to his apartment building in relative silence, except for the fox's panting. He was sure he hadn't lost a lot of blood, but the dizziness was an excuse to let the bear help him.

Luckily the elevator had been fixed a few days ago, so they could go up to the eleventh floor without stumbling up the stairs. He unlocked his apartment and gestured for the bear to go in first. He locked it behind him, and pointed to the kitchen.

"There's a first aid kit in there," Carson said. "Can you grab it?" He went ahead and sat down on the couch, carefully untying the jacket around his arm.

Well, it wasn't completely destroyed. It was mainly just scraping and gravel, which he started gingerly picking out. The jacket was definitely ruined, so he just set the chips on the bloody fabric.

"I will take care," Peter said, kneeling down in front of him. He was only a few inches taller than the fox, but near twice as wide. His fingers were gentle, though, using the tweezers included in the kit to pick away the road dirt, and rinsing off with one of Carson's kitchen towels. The fox tried not to wince, since this wasn't the first time a car had hit him—it was a peril of riding a bike in St. Marx—but it was the first time someone else had taken care of him. He kept his eyes on the bear's face, but Peter kept his eyes fixedly on the scrapes along the fox's arm, finishing his care by wrapping Carson's forearm in gauze. Carson had a small scrape on his paw as well, which the bear took and carefully cleaned as well.

"How do you feel?" Peter asked. The fox blushed under his fur; the bear wasn't letting his paw go, the rough fingers very gently caressing the palm of his paw.

"Better," he said, looking away. He felt the bear lean up, and could see Peter's face out of the corner of his eye. The other male's breath gently tickled the side of his muzzle.

Something pressed into his covered paw, and he glanced over. Peter had given him back his broken cell phone, with the app still up under the cracked glass. His daily list of local hookups was up, showing a dozen different sets of abs and more private areas.

"You call me when you get it fixed, yes? I pay for it. And the bike," Peter said. He gently kissed the fox on the cheek, eliciting more blushing and a little tail wag. Well, that was nice. He felt a little pressure on his bandage, and looked over. The bear was writing a phone number on it.

"Ok," Carson said. The bear squeezed his good paw and give him another kiss on the cheek.

"You are very cute." With the accent, it sounded more like a statement of fact than a compliment. Carson smiled.

"I'll get it replaced today," he whispered.

The bear left the apartment, leaving the fox a little time to calm down and change his clothes. He needed to spray a little cologne to cover up the scent of arousal, and a long-sleeve shirt for the bandages. It wasn't like he could text his boss to say why he was going to be late to work.

It took him another half an hour in a cab to make it to Bookkeepers, the bookstore he worked at, but luckily he had enough cash on him.

When he showed the bandage to his boss, there wasn't much of an argument either, since the lion knew the dangers of riding a bike in town. Carson had a new employee to tutor, and he needed to set up one of the new romance racks. They'd gotten in another rack of tiny novels with ridiculously attractive guys holding swooning middle-aged vixens and lionesses in corsets.

"What should I do?" a young coyote asked. He was lanky and wore a polo shirt with a hand-written nametag reading 'Richard'. If this wasn't his first job, Carson would be really surprised.

"Just pass me the stacks from the boxes," the fox said. The coyote wagged his tail and started doing what he was told.

"Is there any special way we have to do this?" Richard asked. Carson sighed.

"Just make sure the same books go into the same stack, and try and keep the pornier ones on the highest shelves so kids don't grab them," Carson said.

"How do I tell?" the coyote asked.

"Flip it open. If you see the words 'cock' or 'hungry pussy', it goes on the top."

Richard blushed.

"We need to work on the kid's section after this. They always tear it up."

He spent the next few hours getting Richard more familiar with where each section was. The coyote had shopped here before, but never for art reference or children's literature. On lunch, Carson walked over to the phone store and waited for the one gay tech to find him a new phone and transfer over the data. When the new one turned on, it immediately beeped—apparently the badger tech was not only gay, but also amazingly well-endowed. Carson browsed through his pictures, smiling at the tech before going back to the bookstore. He sent a text to Peter after stepping in the bathroom to check the number on his arm.

*Got it replaced. Cost $227.14.*

He went to a shelf to organize until his phone buzzed.

*No problem. Would you like to get together tonight?*

Well, that did sound good, though he wasn't really looking for someone to date. While he shifted a stack of magazines with one paw he typed with the other.

*My place?*
*No problem. Be there at 7. I will bring pizza for after.*
He needed to pop into the bathroom and give himself another spritz of cologne.

Even if the bear had already seen his apartment, Carson took the time to do laundry, wash the dishes, and put away the Blu-rays he'd left on the coffee table. He made sure he had some coffee, and when he heard a knock at the door, he double-checked the drawer in the bedside table to make sure he didn't need to go buy lube. The fox brushed down the fur along his muzzle when the intercom buzzed, and he let the bear into the building. It only took a few minutes for him to make it to Carson's front door.

Peter had changed into a black tracksuit that almost perfectly matched his fur, and carried two pizzas and a bottle of wine in his paws. Carson stepped aside and let the bear into the apartment, shutting the door behind him. The bear walked straight into the kitchen, setting the pizzas on the counter and putting the wine in the fridge. He turned back toward the fox, waiting until Carson followed him into the kitchen. Two large paws slid around the fox's waist, and even if the scent of the pizza enticed him after all his housework, the scent of the bear did so even more. Peter pressed closer, kissing him on the cheek, and then moved a bit to kiss him full on the lips.

"I look at your profile," Peter said once he broke the kiss, paws sliding down to the fox's rump. "It gives me many ideas."

Carson tilted his head up as the bear nibbled down the side of his muzzle and across his throat. His arm still stung, but that wasn't going to stop this from happening. His sheath already bulged, and he could smell that the bear didn't plan on waiting either. One of the bear's paws lifted up his shirt, and after it ended up on the kitchen floor, the powerful jaws nipped at his throat, making him yelp and his member jump out of his sheath.

"It said you would like that," he growled. One paw roamed up his chest and gripped one of his nipples. He practically squeaked, and he knew the front of his boxers were no longer dry.

"And that."

Carson was glad he'd put the information up there, since it made sure less time was spent in person, but it was rare someone pushed his buttons immediately.

He reached a paw down, and found the bear was already fully hard in his tracksuit pants. He squeezed the length through the cloth, his own cock getting harder at feeling how thick it was. It would fit, since the bear didn't have a knot, but it would be a hell of a ride. He'd fooled around with bears a couple of times, since there were some on the app, but they were rare enough to be a treat. One of the bear's paws touched his bandaged arm.

"I take care of you tonight," Peter said. "You not have to do anything."

The bear dropped to his knees, and before the fox could say anything else, his pants were unbuttoned and hot breath brushed his length. He wagged his tail as two big paws gripped his hips, lips wrapping around the head of his cock. Panting, he placed both his paws on the bear's head. Peter hadn't undressed at all yet, and here the fox was, naked from the waist up with his pants open. It was a hell of an apology for clipping him with his car.

He couldn't help but thrust forward when the bear started sucking. Peter wasn't great, but he was good enough, bobbing and swirling his tongue while one paw wrapped around the base of the fox's cock behind his knot. He squeezed. As much as the fox wanted to arch his back and just pound away, he tried to stay fairly still, watching the bear bob his head, twisting his muzzle this way and that, only occasionally pulling off to breathe. One time when he did, a spurt of the fox's precum landed on the bear's nose, and he just slurped it off and went back down on him.

It had been a few days since he'd taken care of himself, so it didn't take long for the fox to feel that familiar pressure start to build up. Reluctantly, he pulled the bear's muzzle off, watching him lick his lips.

"I don't wanna pop just yet," he said, and the bear took the hint. He stood back up, the front of his pants practically soaked.

"Show me to bedroom," Peter said, and the fox took his paw, his other holding up his pants so he wouldn't trip.

He'd changed the sheets too, which was good, since as soon as they crossed the threshold into the room, the bear turned him around, kissed him full on the lips, and then pushed him back on the bed. Huge paws yanked his pants and boxers off, leaving him naked. However, the bear didn't strip—instead, he pulled his track pants down just enough so the elastic snapped under his balls. God, he was big, he wasn't wearing underwear, and his cock leaked like crazy. Peter crawled up on the bed, pushing the fox further up with his knees. He felt the weight of the length sliding between his cheeks, and he moaned, reaching over and opening the drawer of the bedside table. Peter noticed, and pulled out the bottle of lube.

If a guy was leaking a lot, Carson might have tried without lube, but there was no way Peter would fit without assistance. The bear popped open the top, first pouring some on the fox's length, stroking him while he got himself ready. He couldn't really wrap his legs around the bear, since he was so big, so he just spread as much as possible. The head of the bear's cock pressed into his tailhole, and he then started to guide it in with one paw.

Carson kept breathing evenly and tried to stay relaxed. He involuntarily clenched a few times, but the bear just kept sinking into him. It felt so good to be filled. For some reason, the vast majority of the people on Knotz were bottoms, which gave him precious little choice in being plowed. Peter stopped moving and leaned down over the fox. The bear's paw left his length, lifting Carson's arms over his head and gripping his wrists. Peter's gaze was on his face, making sure it was alright. When Carson didn't say anything, because he knew it said 'likes to cum paw-free if possible' in his profile, the bear started rocking his hips.

God, this was great. When he hooked up with a top canine, nine times out of ten the wolf or dog would just start pounding away, nipping, barking, growling, and trying to tie and cum as fast as possible. There were times Carson liked that, but right now, especially since the day had started with him being hit by a car, being slowly taken was heavenly. He wasn't exactly worn out, since he was rock-hard and definitely going to pop in the next few minutes, but it was nice to feel the bear slowly pull back, then powerfully thrust back in, making sure he felt every inch. Peter's belly also rubbed against his cock, which felt pretty damn amazing.

When Peter started to speed up, the fox started letting out little yipping noises, urging him on. Carson was close, and he couldn't

13

last any longer. The paws holding his wrists squeezed tighter, the thrusts started getting ragged, and the fox's toes curled. With the bear panting over him, he yelped as he came all over his own belly, the bear slamming into him the whole time, the shots making a mess of his fur and the bear's jacket. A few more thrusts and the bear gritted his teeth, holding his breath as he pushed in deep as he could go, and Carson felt him pulse and shoot inside him. They'd almost been completely in sync, and now they were both spent, breathing hard, and sticky.

Peter pulled out, making the fox gasp, and the bear rolled over on the bed, pulling his track pants back over his groin. It was definitely wet, but the fox guessed he just didn't care right now. Carson sighed happily, closing his eyes for a second just to bask in the afterglow. He heard a shuffling, and the sound Knotz made when turning on: it was a wolf howl.

"I made profile. You show me how to link to you, yes?"

The fox took the phone from Peter's paw, lazily typing in his info into the "Repeat 'O' ffenders" list. Those lists were private and showed distance and availability for those people immediately without having to go through more menus. He let Peter do the same to his phone.

"I bring you new bike tomorrow morning," Peter said. "When is next day you want to do this?" Well, Carson appreciated someone who wasn't going to bullshit around. The bear had hit him with his car, found out he was gay because of his broken phone, and they'd enjoyed a good fuck. What more could a fox ask for?

"How about on Saturday? I don't work then," the fox said, rolling out of bed. The pizza was probably cold, but he had a microwave for a reason. When he opened the pizza box, there were a few bills and coins tucked under one slice. It was more than enough money for the phone.

They ate in relative silence, with paws only occasionally roaming. He found it odd the bear hadn't stripped down, but maybe he had some embarrassing scar or piercing he didn't want to show off. Some guys were like that. Carson worked out a lot, and he was glad to let people see.

Peter left the wine closed, and left with one more kiss on the cheek, having only eaten two pieces of pizza. When he was about to

14

go, he took off his jacket and wrapped it around his waist, hiding his wet crotch from view. Well, Carson had a new fuck-buddy. When he checked his phone, he noticed the bear had also put a new number in his contacts under just 'Peter'. That would help once the bandages came off.

Perhaps fucking while having his arm wrapped up in bandages wasn't the best of ideas, since now that his euphoria was going down he noticed he'd started to bleed again. None of the scratches were very deep, so he kept it unwrapped while he took a shower, cleaned the area, and re-wrapped his arm. While he brushed out his fur, he switched on his television. He didn't recognize the sitcom, but *Grown-ups and Boys*, one he liked, was on after it according to a commercial. He flopped down onto the couch and unlocked his phone while the show progressed through the opening credits.

It might be a stupid show about immature new husbands, but it served as good background noise while he flipped through Knotz profiles. There were a few wolves in leather within a block of him, but he wasn't necessarily a fan. Too many liked to establish the alpha/omega role, and he just wanted to do some fucking or get fucked. Sure, he had some subby quirks and turn-ons, but he didn't want to completely submit. A few foxes within a mile, and that was fun, since there were times he wanted someone about his own size to fool around with. A cute black cat hadn't included a cock pic, but instead chose a classy pinup pose for his profile. The fox added him to his list of 'maybes'. When the app refreshed the list, a Rottweiler popped up in his building. He added him to the list, as well a handsome ram who had 'total bottom' as his listed position. There were those times he just wanted to pound someone bigger than him.

He had to be at work at open tomorrow, but that didn't stop him from watching a few more hours of television. When he felt his eyes getting heavier, he rolled over, pulled one of the pillows under his head, and yanked a fleece blanket out from under the couch. Right now, he just didn't feel like changing the sheets.

His phone's alarm went off far too early in the morning, and too late, the fox remembered he had slept on the couch. He rolled over, falling right on the floor and banging his funny bone. Cursing,

15

he checked to make sure the bandages were fine and found some clothes. His bedroom reeked of sex, but he could wait to deal with that until he got home. A clean pair of pants, a tight t-shirt, and a sweater and he was ready to go out the door when he heard a buzz at the intercom. Who would call this early?

"Yes?" the fox said into the speaker.

"I have a delivery from Mr. Belov," a British voice said. When Carson didn't answer immediately, the voice added, "Mr. Peter Belov."

"I'm coming down," he answered.

Waiting for him at the building's entrance was a bull terrier wearing a suit, complete with tails and a cane in one paw. The second paw held up a new bicycle of a much, much more expensive brand than the fox had been riding yesterday morning. He practically drooled. Also, parked on the street in front of the meter was a real, honest-to-God limousine.

"This is for me to...borrow?" He asked.

"No, sir," the dog said. "This is from Mr. Belov."

"To keep?"

"Yes, sir."

"I...I should call him about this," the fox said.

"Mr. Belov is still asleep. I would advise against it."

Why was he freaking out about this? Peter had destroyed his other bike, and had now replaced it. Maybe he didn't know bikes, and just went to a store and picked the one that he thought looked like his old one and with a price that matched his guilt. Or his sexual satisfaction. Or both. Carson took a deep breath. He needed a new bike, and here it was. He could deal with the minutiae of the situation later.

"Thank you..."

"Marshall, sir," the bull terrier said, taking the hint. "If you do not need anything else, I will be going."

"Thank you, Marshall, for running down here this early." God, he was bad at conversation. Was it all the texting? However, the dog smiled.

"No problem, sir."

Carson got on the bike, a little bit of a nervous wreck with all the people walking by staring at Marshall, and started pedaling down the road to work.

Damn, the ride on this bike was smoother than he'd dreamed. It was still a bike, which meant lots of weaving through traffic and narrowly missing being hit by opened doors, but he was used to all of that. As long as no one tried to beat a red light or turn too quickly, he'd be fine. His luck probably wouldn't go poorly two days in a row. Well, getting fucked after getting clipped by a car might count as a mixed bag.

Only Terrence, the store manager, was already there, so while the lion filled the registers, the fox locked up his new bike, then powered up and logged into all the computers. He didn't need to dress too fancy for this job, since apparently customers were put off when someone in customer service dressed like a lawyer. Terrence, however, dressed like he owned the place.

"Did you get all the new romances out?" Terrence asked as he filled the central register. He was very tall, and nearly as wide, though it was all muscle.

"Yup."

"We got another few boxes of them in the last delivery. I want you and Richard to have them all up by noon," Terrence said. Carson liked working for Terrence. There was no bullshit with him.

"No problem. Did we get the new Patrick Pratt in?" He was a steamy thriller writer all the middle-aged women came in to buy. Carson's mom had a few signed first editions.

"Should be here in the first delivery," Terrence said as he finished up with the cash. "Make sure the guy doesn't miss one of the boxes again. I don't want customer complaints."

About half an hour later, the delivery truck showed up. The normal driver, a cute husky, must be off today, so Carson stayed on business with his female replacement. Come to think of it, the last time they'd been shorted Patrick Pratt books was when that husky had fucked him in the back of the truck. Maybe having a female driver wasn't a bad thing.

Doors opened at eight, and a few people milled in almost immediately. The attached coffee shop was most of it, though that meant people at least had to look at books this early in the morning. A few would buy the new releases or bestsellers, though almost no one walked back to the customer service desk to ask about some rare or off-the-wall book. Richard and Sarah both clocked in as the smell of fresh coffee filled the building.

"This is my last day," Sarah commented as she pulled the first cart of books from the back.

"Why's that?" Carson asked. Sarah quitting would mean more work for him, both in more shifts and in training someone else new.

"Boyfriend got a better job upstate," she said as she started refilling the shelves.

"What are you going to do?" he asked.

"Get married," she said. Carson didn't really consider that an adequate answer, but he figured she could do whatever the hell she wanted.

Richard went to putting up the rest of the romances, while Carson started rearranging the new release wall to fit the new Pratt, *Bone To Pick*. That stupid vampire book had to go back to its own section— he was surprised so many gay guys liked a book with no gay people in it. He put it back in the adult mystery section, shifting everything to put *Bone to Pick* at the top of the shelf. Almost as soon as they were in sight, people started to reach over him, taking copies to the coffee register.

"Do you know what the one before this is?" one of the elderly vixens asked. There was a group of older vixens here once a week. He gently took the book from her paws, and opened it to the 'Other Thrillers by Patrick Pratt' page.

"What was the last one you read?" he asked. She looked down the list and pointed to *Bonemeal*.

"Ok, there are two other books between that one and *Bone to Pick*. Would you like me to find those for you?" Carson asked. He looked up—Terrence was helping one of the others in the vixen pack.

"Oh, thank you," she said. "Paperback, please." That answered his next question.

After the vixens left, the second morning stream of people started. These were housewives or people who worked an afternoon shift, here for a little bit of peace in their lives. The moms went straight to the kids section, tugging toddlers past all the more mature material. Those without children perused the slutty romances. Some of them hit on Richard, and it was really easy to see him blush. Carson's phone buzzed as he finished up on the front shelves.

*Was the bike good?* The text read.

*A lot better than the one I had.* The fox sent back. He was a master of texting while working.

*I think Saturday will be fun.* The next text from Peter read. The bear had been a hell of a ride. The next few days would indeed be fun.

# Chapter Two: SlinkyOne21 and Beef4767

Richard adapted well, since despite what a lot of people thought, there really wasn't a constant stream of busywork to do in a bookstore. Carson helped him stack the book carts correctly to move product from the back of the store to the front, and learn which employee knew which department best, but other than that, the coyote spent most of the day walking around and asking customers if they needed any help. Since Carson wasn't a cashier, the only time he touched a computer that wasn't his phone was to look up a product. Most young customers were just here to browse to find stuff they'd buy later online, but he didn't mind that the same way the store manager did. Of course, he had a completely selfish reason for not caring: this was the closest bookstore to Papillon, the gayborhood.

Guys walked in and out all the time, dressed in mesh shirts and tight pants. A good many of them were on their phones, doing the same thing Carson did on his breaks—looking for people to fuck. Sometimes, he would be sitting in the café, sipping a coffee and watching as some cute guy's phone beeped, and he looked over to smile or wag his tail.

*Work here?* A message from Knotz asked. It was the cute ferret waiting for his coffee a few feet away. Well, Carson only knew that because he could guess that the ass in the picture matched the one in the jeans in front of him.

*On break.* He replied. The ferret's small fingers worked over a touchscreen while Carson took another sip. The guy was obviously nervous, but cute, and barely five feet tall, wearing a sweatshirt against the chilly day but not bothering with looser-fitting pants. The fox wondered if he lived close by.

*After work, you wanna do something?* Came the next message. He smiled. The kid didn't really know how Knotz worked. You messaged someone logged in as 'Available', since that meant they were ready to go to either person's apartment or condo right now and fuck. There was a reason the fox's profile right now was set to 'Later'. However, the ferret was cute, and he was in the mood for someone smaller than him today.

*Are you legal?* Carson asked. When he watched the message pop up, the ferret didn't bristle; he just sighed. Sure, the ferret looked nervous, but that was probably from a lack of experience with hookups rather than being jailbait.

*Then be at the Hager Apartment Building at 330.* The fox typed in. Now he had something to look forward to after work.

Richard was quietly filling the magazine racks when Carson came back from break. The task always got left to the newest person, because it was pretty mindless. The coyote kept bending down, running his fingers down the ledge to find the right space, all while lazily wagging his tail. He was terribly cute, but Carson wasn't sure if he was someone who just happened to live near Papillon or was actually part of the community. Also, he wasn't sure if it was kosher to fuck coworkers. There'd been Rob a few months ago, but that had been on the down-low, and in the backroom, after hours. He figured it would be more difficult for a younger guy to keep a secret. Rob had just been horny, and there was just something really hot about getting fucked between piles of books. It brought back college fantasies.

"How can I help you?" he asked, refocusing on the surrounding customers and automatically fixing his smile. A young goat stood in front of his desk. Shit. He wasn't good with children. This one was maybe eight or nine; he also wasn't very good at guessing ages.

"I need this," the goat said, passing a piece of paper across the counter to him.

"*Rotations* by Charle Du Mond..." Carson muttered as he typed everything in the computer and waited for the connection to notice. They really needed to finish upgrading the building's electronics. "It looks like we have copies in hardback and paperback. Is this for your mom or dad?" He doubted a kid wanted a book on international environmental policies.

"My dad," the goat said. "He's over there." The kid pointed to the sci-fi aisle. Carson could just make out a pair of horns over the shelves.

"I'll go find it," the fox said, leaning against the desk. "You go tell your dad I'll have it here at the desk, alright?"

"Ok," the kid said, then started to wander away. Carson watched the higher-up horns move, indicating the older goat was watching where his son was going. That was better than a lot of parents.

It took him a few minutes to find the book for the goat, which he set on the customer service counter while he checked the shipments for the next few days. A few more children's books were being restocked tomorrow, and several boxes of paperback mysteries. Those were constant sellers. Carson wondered if lesbians liked murder mysteries, and then wondered if that was homophobic.

The goat retrieved his book, choosing the hardcover, and walked toward the front of the store. A Persian cat needed to find a specific art book for her grandson, so the fox helped her next. She was followed by a parent tugging two toddlers needing to know when the employee who read children's books at lunchtime would be back. He'd been fired for stealing, but the fox just told her that he'd been transferred, and that they were looking for a replacement.

When he got off work, he wondered how many pings Knotz would get on the ride home. As an experiment, he set his status to 'Available' and started pedaling. Everyone around here was well-dressed, and most people were fit, so there was no way to tell. It was only a twenty minute bike ride home, and a lot smoother than on his previous model. He'd have to ask Peter where he'd purchased it in case it needed a repair down the road. However, the frame felt like solid metal, and it was definitely twice as heavy to pick up. Another clip might not even dent it.

The ferret was pacing outside his building when the fox got there, playing on his phone. A few other people were definitely checking him out, and Carson hopped off the bike and guided it into the bike rack, locking it in place. Peter had even purchased him a more secure chain and lock. When he checked his phone, he noticed he was a few minutes late, and that Knotz had picked up damn near a hundred people on his route home.

"C'mon in," he said. The ferret jumped a little and turned around. When he saw it was the fox, he relaxed and held open the door. Damn, he was skinny up close. Once they were in the elevator, Carson noticed the other guy kept moving. It was little things, like rubbing his paws together or flicking his tail, but he never seemed to stop. The elevator was slow today, so Carson decided to liven things up.

One paw was all it took to make the ferret damn near jump out of his fur. That paw might have been on his groin, but they were about to fuck. Random touching shouldn't be an issue. Carson squeezed the ferret's package through his jeans, feeling him almost instantly get hard.

"Don't tell me your name," the fox said, suddenly pressing the ferret against the side of the small elevator, Carson's paw now stroking him through his pants and the fox's lips blowing into one of his small ears. "Just say top or bottom." He'd read the kid's profile already, but he wanted to be told. Carson could see the blush under the ferret's tan fur, but he also felt the hard cock between his fingers and knew which was going to win.

"B...b...bottom," the ferret said.

"Ok."

Carson's apartment was the closest to the elevator, and luckily there was no one in the hallway as he pulled the nervous ferret into his apartment. He shut the door behind him and pushed the smaller guy up against the door, shucking his pants down. The ferret gasped, and when Carson wrapped a paw around his length and started stroking, he started breathing heavier. Carson's phone buzzed, and he quickly checked it. It was a text from Peter, but it could wait. He pulled the ferret's shirt up and off, throwing it to the side and helping his new conquest step out of everything below the waist. He was skinny, a bit too skinny by the fox's standards, but he was blushing all the way from his ears to his throat.

One big advantage of being strong and skinny is people don't expect it. Carson picked the naked ferret up, and ignoring the squeak, carried him to the couch, leaving the pile of clothes behind. Whenever Carson worked out, even if it was just a normal bike ride, it always left him hornier than usual. He peeled off his work clothes and climbed onto the couch, straddling the ferret. The ferret breathed fast, and it was cute to watch the little guy pant. Carson ran his paws down the ferret's chest. His scent was sharp, normal for a mustelid, but Carson liked it. He settled between the ferret's legs, brushing his tail aside to expose his tailhole.

"Reach over there and hand me the bottle of lube," Carson said. The ferret looked at the coffee table, blinked a few times, and passed it over. The fox was horny, and he didn't want to wait, so he immediately lubed up a finger and started probing. The ferret jumped a little, tensed, and then spread his legs a little more. His tiny paws gripped the fox's arm, but didn't stop him. Carson didn't plan to slow down now. He pulled his paw back, grabbed his own cock, and started to press in, lifting the ferret's legs and bending them so his knees nearly touched his chest. Thanks to all the lube, the fox slipped in easily, though he heard the ferret hiss.

"Put your paws behind your knees and hold 'em," he said. The ferret did as he was told, and that gave the fox the leverage he needed. He pulled back, keeping one paw on the ferret's cock and the other around his own knot, since he had no plans to tie right now.

He started really giving the kid a pounding, and dammit if it wasn't cute. Normally that wasn't a word he associated with fucking, but with each thrust the ferret let out a little squeak, still covered in a blush, and with his eyes squinted shut. It took him no time at all to let out a little whimper, rock his head back against the side of the couch, and to start spraying cum all over the fox's paw. Carson growled at the sudden tightness, squeezing his knot hard and giving a few more thrusts before he filled the ferret with cum. The fox pulled out almost immediately. Standing up, he pointed at one of the closed doors.

"Bathroom's right there," he said, and the ferret, out of breath, nodded and rolled off the couch. While he stumbled away, the fox walked into his master bathroom to clean up. Carson took a little longer than he really needed, but he wanted to wait to see what the ferret did. He heard his front door open and shut—yup, the ferret understood what a hookup meant. No talking, no conversation, and no bullshit. He walked out, pulled his pants back on, and checked his phone.

Peter had sent him a cock pic, with the message 'not posting this public'. He must have started editing his profile on Knotz. Carson had more than enough on there to let anyone know whether or not they were going to hook up: turn-ons, turn-offs, along with pictures of his cock and ass. He kept the list of people he'd hooked up with before private, and the repeatable list for when he didn't want to roll the dice for a good lay. There was a wolf investment banker a few streets down who always had nights free, so any day he wanted to be tied, he could. Guy didn't talk, just stripped and starting thrusting. Carson could appreciate that. Since the wolf always came to the fox's place, he strongly suspected the other canid was married. He didn't want to ask, because if he knew the wolf was, he would stop hooking up with him, and the wolf had a big cock.

Someone knocked on his door and made him jump. No one came to visit him, especially not in the middle of the afternoon. It only took a second to get his shirt back on before he was able to answer the door.

"Hi, mom," Carson said.

"God, this place always smells like sex," she said, though with a smile.

"You just missed him. Cute, too."

His mom dressed like every other hippie in St. Marx—jeans and a spaghetti strap shirt that bared just a little midriff. She was in good shape, since she jogged everywhere. After setting a brown paper bag down that smelled like Chinese food, she kissed him on the cheek.

"Go wash up and I'll pull down some plates. You smell like ferret cum." Well, there was no arguing with that.

After washing his paws, Carson and his mom sat down to some pork dumplings and rice. His mom always used chopsticks, and he always used a fork, since in his opinion, food tasted the same both ways and he didn't want to be frustrated. This must be a new fast food place, since the dumplings were greasier than he liked.

"How's your job been doing?" she asked.

"I'm floor manager. Means I get the new people in line, show customers where books are," Carson said

"That's what you did before."

"Yeah, but now they're paying me for it."

"Oh."

They ate in silence for a few minutes before his mom brought up a normally-forbidden topic, or after Carson thought about it for a second, a topic only his mom ever brought up.

"Have you found anyone to date?"

"Have you?" Carson retorted. In a more conservative city, his mom might be considered slutty, but here, her boyfriends and one-night-stands over the years barely stood out.

"I'll have you know I'm dating a nice fox I met at the gym," she said before grabbing another dumpling. "He's a teacher at PS 135."

"That's my high school," Carson muttered. He went down a mental checklist of attractive, male fox teachers he knew about. Only one came to mind, but he was gay, something his mom did not need to know about from him interning there in college.

"He wasn't there when you were," his mom added. Well, that made sure that Mr. Gonzales wasn't bisexual, and set to bed the horrifying thought of him and his mom having been with the same guy.

"I've got a...few options," Carson said. A few hundred options, actually.

"Someone for more than an hour?"

That took the fox a bit longer to think about, since he decided he didn't want to go into a protracted argument with his mom. If he didn't give her a single person, she would start recommending her gay neighbors, which were most of them. He remembered every hookup, but she remembered every available homosexual male looking for a relationship.

"A bear I met riding to work," Carson said, which was technically true.

"What's his name?"

"What's your boyfriend's name?" he countered.

"Elian," she said. Damn. He'd been hoping she wouldn't tell him.

"Peter. He's Russian, I think."

"Ooo, sexy accent. Is he a fat bear or a muscly bear?"

"A little of both," Carson said.

"You should see if he can bench-press you. That's always fun."

"I don't even know if he works out," the younger fox said.

His mom swallowed a mouthful of rice. "What does he do for a living?"

"EMT," Carson lied. His mom smiled. Since he kept getting clipped or shoved off his bike, dating someone who could patch him up would be a boon.

"You get hit again?" she asked. In the past year he'd sprained a wrist or ankle three times.

He pulled up his sleeve to show her his arm. She made typical sympathetic mother noises, which reminded him he needed to change out of his work clothes. Another text message buzzed as he walked into his bedroom, but he ignored it. His mom didn't like cell phones, or really any technology.

"You still using that app for cock?" she asked through the bedroom door.

Carson paused, a t-shirt halfway down his chest. How did she know about that? Come to think of it, the developer made one for straight hookups called Barbz, but he couldn't visualize his mom using a smartphone for anything, let alone to find sex.

"There's nothing wrong with it," he replied.

"You know, they might last more than an hour if you had something to talk about. Books, movies, something like that."

"What?" Carson said. "My job is to talk to people about books. I don't want to do it in my free time."

"I'm not talking about 'Did you get the new Pratt in?' talking about books," his mom said as he stepped into a pair of shorts. "I'm talking the 'what's your favorite Shakespeare' or 'aren't modern vampires pussies' kind of talking about books, cupcake. Stuff people talk about."

"What's your favorite Shakespeare, then?" he asked as he walked back into the kitchen. He opened the fridge and popped open a Diet Coke.

"*Twelfth Night*," his mom said. She pulled a glass from the cabinet and filled it from the faucet. She didn't drink anything processed, which seemed stupid to him, since she'd just eaten Chinese fast food. He supposed she picked her battles in a modern world.

"*Midsummer Night's Dream*," he said. She stuck out her tongue at him.

"You're such a fag."


Once she left, he went through the messages. He'd forgotten to log out of Knotz before answering the door, so he had two new propositions. The rabbit was cute, but he felt sated for the moment, and he just didn't like hooking up with beavers. He could deal with musk, but a beaver's scent was just ridiculously strong unless they fucked right after a shower. The last message was from Peter.

*Making sure you are still free tomorrow,* it read. He'd forgotten it was already Friday.

*After eight. Someone quit, so I had to take their days.* He texted back.

*I will send Marshall to pick you up. Do you want him to get you from work or apartment?* Came a reply. Since he still wasn't sure if he wanted the bear to know where he worked, the answer was easy.

*I'll need to shower and such before we have our fun.* Apartment. He sent.

*I will have him be there about nine. Is that OK?* The fox's fingers paused on the screen.

*That should be fine. Gives me time to eat.* Was it evil of him to hint? The reply came back very fast.

*I have dessert planned. Something very unique.* Well, that sounded reasonable. The idea of Marshall cooking for them kind of freaked him out. His mom wasn't poor by any means, but they'd never been 'We have Help' rich.

*Sounds delicious.*

*Something other than you.* Peter replied. The fox smirked.

*Promises, Promises.* He sent back.

Would it be good to see the bear again? They certainly clicked between the sheets—or more specifically, on top of them—and he wondered after the conversation with his mom if he could talk to Peter about anything significant. He didn't really know what the other guy did for a living, but maybe he liked stupid movies or fantasy books. They might not be Carson's favorite, but he could definitely talk about them forever. There were authors he knew by heart, and as off-the-wall as it was, his mom did have a point; everyone knew a least a little about Shakespeare. Maybe Peter thought he was gay, or that a noble had actually written the plays. Carson didn't believe any of that crap, but it was fun to debate.

Now that he thought about it, he never talked about anything controversial with anyone he slept with. Politics or religion just weren't things that entered conversation when you took somebody's pants off. Sometimes he saw a cross or a Star of David on a necklace, but he never asked about it. Topics like that made people uncomfortable, and definitely were bonerkills. He didn't want that to happen. Movies were always a possibility. Maybe they could watch a movie between sessions, or as foreplay. It couldn't hurt anything.

*What's your favorite Shakespeare play?* Carson texted to Peter.

*Coriolanus.* Read Peter's text.

*Never heard of that one.* He sent back.

*It's about naked roman generals.* Peter sent.

*I don't think that's what it's about :P.* was his answer. How could a Shakespeare play just be about beefcake?

*There's politics and fighting and revenge and all, but I like watching the naked Romans. Last time I saw it was all naked wolves on stage.* Well, he'd heard of Macbeth completely naked, but this had so much more appeal. Did they perform it around here?

There were still a few hours of daylight, so the fox went for a ride. He liked cycling, not just because it helped him stay healthy and kept his expenses down, but because there was a sense of freedom he didn't associate with driving. Pedestrians needed to push and shove through intersections. On a good day, he could glide through traffic when it was at a standstill. The mayor had been trying to get bike lanes approved, but the city council thought it would be too expensive. Carson secretly thought it was because the mayor was gay and the city council didn't like that, even if St. Marx was a remarkably progressive place.

He passed the local grocery store and a salon, but when he saw his gym he glided into the parking lot. This was another building always full of cute guys, because being gay in the big city meant being a perfect ten to a lot of people. Carson was fine with his build, but lifting some weights never hurt. There were also yoga classes, which the instructors realized people took for the increased flexibility rather than the inner peace.

"Hey," the fox said, pulling his membership card out of his wallet as he walked into the entryway. There was a muscle-bound bull at the desk, ready to act as security as much as secretary.

"Hey, Carson," he said. Apparently the bull remembered him, though for the life of him the fox couldn't remember the bull's name. Shower sex tended to obscure his memory.

The fox chose a simple weight regimen to spend the next hour. His legs got more than enough work, between riding around the city and fucking bunnies, but his upper body needed to keep up the strength training. If he expected to surprise more guys by carrying them around, he needed to make sure his body was up for it. A few reps in and he hit his stride, switching between a few different machines to be able to people-watch as much as vary his workout.

The gym was always packed with all sorts of species, so whatever Carson was in the mood for, he could oogle. A pair of rats jogged on two matching treadmills. A group of wolves and cats chatted while slowly pedaling stationary bikes. The fox stood by the idea that if you could talk about what movie you wanted to see this weekend, you weren't working out hard enough. A few of the weight machines were occupied by those kinds of people that considered exercise a game they could win, and kept egging each other on and flexing. It was fun to watch, but those kinds of people only ever hooked up with each other.

"Want a spotter?" someone asked as the fox settled on a weight bench. When Carson looked up, he smiled at the bull from the front desk. Well, he smiled at the bull from the front desk's package a few inches from his nose.

"Sure," he said. The fox placed his paws in position. How would this play out?

They started on simple eighty-pound reps, slowly moving up to one hundred and thirty. He could do two hundred pounds without much of an issue, but he didn't want to show off right now, especially if he might need the strength in his arms later this afternoon. He started to work up a sweat, and would definitely need to hit the showers before he left. He set the bar back on the rack and sat up. When he did, he heard his phone buzz, and a little howl come from the bull's pocket.

"I need to shower," Carson said. As he stood up, he brushed a paw over the bull's pocket and poked the covered cell phone with one finger.

Like the fox expected, the bull followed him into the showers. Carson liked how this place was set up—some of the shower stalls gave a little privacy by separating them from the main locker room with a solid door, since he suspected he was not the only one to shower with someone else. He turned on the hot water while he pulled off his shirt and pants, setting them in a basket attached to the wall. When he turned around, he watched the bull doing the same thing.

"I assume you're on break?" he asked as he pulled the shower curtain back and stepped in under the flow, slicking his fur down. The bull was all muscle, and his fur was short enough that even before he stepped into the shower stall, a small bottle in one huge paw, the fox could appreciate his built physique.

"I can take my lunch early," he said before pulling the curtain back in place.

These stalls were big enough for any of the larger species to shower comfortably, but with the two of them in here, it was tight. Of course, that's exactly what the fox wanted. He turned around, pressing his rump against the bull's rapidly-hardening length. Big paws gripped his hips, and he gripped the handicapped bar. The bull was large—definitely bigger than Peter, and he knew this wasn't the bull's first time in the showers.

The bull took a few minutes just grinding against the fox, getting him hard, reaching a paw around to make sure Carson enjoyed it was well. He appreciated a guy who didn't think the fox needed to take care of himself. He heard the bottle pop through the sound of the rushing water, and after a few seconds, the bull started pressing into him. The head popped in easily, and the length was unrelenting, the bull pressed him against the shower wall as he bottomed out. Carson lifted one leg, setting his foot on the small bench. He knocked over two forgotten bottles of soap, watching them roll against the bull's feet. Every inch of this bull was muscle, and when he started thrusting, the fox needed to brace against the wall just to stay upright.

This wasn't as much sex as it was a pounding. Carson was hard and would definitely get off, but not while his whole mind and body were focused on the huge cock working its way in and out of him. Anyone in less physical shape than him would have had their legs go weak under this kind of assault, but he loved it. Someone this deep in him, without even knowing their name, was what made living here worth the high rent and old, drafty apartment building. A sizeable chunk of the district's populace was available for whenever he wanted someone else for an hour or two. One huge paw on one shoulder, nails digging in, the other stroking him off, and his whole body being rocked with each thrust. This was the life.

He came without even knowing he was working toward it. He just shot cum against the shower wall, the splashes disappearing almost immediately, squeezing hard around the bull inside him. The gym trainer let out a bellow, and he felt the length in him pulse and start to fill him even more. The bull never stopped thrusting, driving the fox to almost howl at the intensity of everything. Taking that ferret earlier today might have been fun, but this was amazing.

When the bull pulled out, the fox slumped against the warm shower wall, taking in a few deep breaths. There was no real time to recover, since almost immediately the bull gave him a light smack on the ass. Carson jumped.

"I think we should work out more often," the bull said.

He stepped out of the showers, and now the fox focused on actually getting the sweat out of his fur. It only took him a few minutes before he switched to the dryers, and after that was done, he stepped back out into the small space between the door and the shower stall. The bull was still there, messing around on his phone, fully dressed.

"I added you," he said, showing Carson his profile page. "Be here same time next week, and I'm sure I can spot you."

While the fox was getting dressed, something occurred to him. Odds were, the bull hooked up with all sorts of people in the gym, and definitely in the shower. If he needed to schedule someone in, that meant a number of cocks the fox couldn't even fathom. People had called him slutty in the past, but a gym trainer who banged regularly on the job was a little bit mind-boggling.

Carson rode back home, pondering what Peter must do on his time off. The fox didn't really have any friends since moving back here, if he didn't count fuck-buddies. Maybe he should find a few who didn't want to suck his cock. Maybe Richard would want to watch television, or whatever it was adult friends did. Back in college it was all weed, rum, and stupid nighttime cartoons. Could he still do that as an adult? Probably not, since dorm life sort of leaned people toward that kind of stuff and his job administered piss tests.

It would make him feel embarrassed to just look up 'how to make friends as an adult,' but maybe he could just look around. Someone who worked at the bookstore had to own a house where they could grill—he'd always liked that. Or a book club. Even with digital readers getting more and more common, surely people still met and discussed books. He imagined a circle of snooty gay foxes, wearing scarves and discussing metaphors, which left him with a goofy smile as he locked up his bike. He could never do that.

# Chapter Three: BlackBearry

Work was always busy on Saturday. Partly, it was because all the offices nearby closed on weekends, and because there was no school. Children swarmed in all sections and aisles, sometimes leaving it to employees to stop them from pulling down copies of *Best Gay Sex Volume Three* or *A Mortician's Assistant*. Carson considered it a parent's responsibility to stop their own children from seeing stuff they didn't like, but a lot of parents felt he was better than a babysitter. Tweens camped in the manga and graphic novel aisle, and even if he had to be careful walking around them, they were quiet and always ended up buying at least a coffee.

Toddlers, however, drove him insane. If they stayed in the kids' corner they weren't his problem, but once unleashed into the rest of the store, they created chaos and headaches. Some pulled down entire shelves just to watch the books fall. Some ripped pages out of whatever they could reach. The worst smeared sticky fingers over everything or poured unattended drinks on displays, causing hundreds of dollars in damage, all because they thought it was funny.

On top of everything, policy said he wasn't allowed to smack them. Carson didn't want to hurt any of the kids—he just wanted their to be repercussions. Anything would have been better than the parents who, after he found wherever they were hiding, accusing *him* of not watching them well enough. If he'd wanted to take care of irate children, he would visit his aunt. She had a brood of little bastards.

"Why do you keep checking your phone?" Richard asked as they cleared some space up front for an author signing. Saturday afternoon always had an appearance by some gay-friendly or children's author.

"Habit," the fox answered. For once, he was keeping Knotz closed, since he knew something fun was going to happen tonight. Really attractive guys kept walking through, some of them checking their phones, but he decided to resist. There was no point in hooking up on his lunch break if it meant he wouldn't be up for the bear tonight. Peter and his time together hadn't been an online hookup, and they had still managed to make a damn fun time of it.

"Are you playing games, or something?" the coyote asked. The fox considered how to answer this.

"Checking the news," he said, keeping his eyes on his paws as he shoved a display a few inches to the left.

"Oh, you have one of those feeds on there?" the coyote asked. He reached into his pocket and showed Carson a phone model he hadn't seen in years. They still sold burn phones? "I can't get anything but texts."

"Don't show that off," Carson said. "People'll think you're a drug dealer."

"Oh…" the canid muttered, pocketing his phone and going back to helping with the display.

"Are you still on your parents' plan, or what?" the fox asked. To his surprise, Richard blushed and folded his ears down.

"I…can't afford a real cell phone."

"Oh," was all Carson could think of saying. Even with roommates, rent in Papillon was obscene. Since he knew the coyote didn't work full-time, it must be tough to afford living here. He must be gay and escaping from some horrible backwards city in the South to tolerate it.

"Well, we get our quarter bonuses on the next paycheck. You could always get one then."

"Wait, what?" The coyote was braced against the bookshelf, ready to move it back a few feet, but now his entire attention focused on the fox.

"Every employee gets a cut of the store's profit every three months. Didn't anyone tell you?" Judging by the kid's stunned expression, no one had.

"I generally use it on booze, but are you old enough?" he ventured. The coyote nodded. Well, that surprised Carson. He'd put the coyote at seventeen or eighteen.

"Then, you want to come get drunk at my place when they come in? I'll help you pick out a real phone. We can watch a movie or something." Well, it was out there. Carson knew adults got drunk together. That counted as socializing.

"Sure," the coyote squeaked out before shaking his muzzle and going back to struggling with the bookcase. Maybe this 'hanging out' thing would work out.

It only took him fifteen minutes to shower and brush out his fur, but a lot longer to pick out something to wear. Normally, he figured they'd be naked in minutes, but since he was going to be picked up in a limo, he wanted to match the part. There wasn't much of a selection in his closet, besides one suit more appropriate for a funeral. Well, he'd bought a few nice ties over the years for job interviews. He decided on some black slacks and a dress shirt, completed with a purple tie. Luckily his arm had healed enough to forego the bandages. One microwaveable pasta dish later and he was ready for some bear fucking.

The intercom buzzer sent him down the stairs, and a minute later he was in the back of the limousine. It had been weird for him that Marshall had waited outside the car to open the door for him, but if he started getting neurotic now it wouldn't stop. Since it was a bit of a drive thanks to afternoon traffic, he decided to try some normal, person-to-person conversation, since the little dividing window between the front seats of the limo and back had been left open.

"How long have you been working for Pe…Mr. Belov?" he asked.

"About three years, sir. Since he moved here, actually,"

"To St. Marx?" Carson asked.

"To the United States, sir."

"Oh." Well, there went his main topic of choice. He went to secondary options.

"Are you his butler?"

"Yes, sir. I cook his meals, I run errands for him, and I fetch things when he requires them."

His curiosity got the better of him. "How often do you…fetch people?"

"Almost every day," Marshall answered promptly. "Mr. Belov generally has me pick up business clients and the like."

"I meant for…this," Carson said, his ears going down a little. Honestly, if this was a regular occurrence, it might make the fox feel better. That would make the bear no different than him, just richer. He'd gotten those pictures, which meant the bear was definitely using Knotz for hookups.

"This would be the first time, sir. As I understand it, there are a few business associates he is…intimate with, but he normally goes to their homes."

That wasn't too bad then. If Peter didn't treat this as something serious, he didn't need to think of it that way.

They pulled up to one of the newest skyscrapers in downtown, and right onto a ramp leading into the basement labeled 'PARKING'. Carson watched as Marshall swiped a card to open the barricade and drove them to one of the closest spots to the elevator. Once they parked, the terrier walked around and opened the door for him.

"I've never been in this building," Carson commented as he stepped out, straightening a wrinkle out of his shirt.

"The Carter Tower is exclusive," Marshall explained. "Mr. Belov had to pay for his suite over two years ago."

"It wasn't finished," the fox said as they stepped into the elevator. He'd made a habit of not biking deep into town until a few months ago, due to the construction.

"That is correct, sir," the dog replied. Alright, the fox had to know. "What does Mr. Belov...do?" Carson asked.

"He is a hedge fund manager," Marshall replied. "Most of those in this building are, sir." Carson didn't really know what that was, except that according to the news they made a crazy amount of money and occasionally were murdered on crime shows for destroying fortunes.

Marshall pressed the button for the sixty-seventh floor, holding it down as he reached into his pocket and retrieved a set of keys, inserting one in a keyhole above the button.

"How many floors are there?" Carson asked.

"Sixty-Eight, sir," Marshall said. Peter must have spent a lot of that hedge money.

Rather than opening on an elaborate hallway or something gilded, the elevator doors opened directly into a suite. Carson had to resist gasping. Most of the living room walls were nothing but windows, one side looking straight down 2nd Avenue all the way to the state capitol building. He stepped into the apartment, dimly noticing the amazingly soft carpet under his feet. His paws met glass and the fox just watched the tiny cars drive down as the lights changed. The state buildings were always illuminated, but he'd never seen them from above. Why had he been worried about coming here? If he'd chickened out, he would have never gotten to see this.

"Like the view?" Peter said.

"Yeah…" the fox said, still transfixed. Arms wrapped around his waist from behind, and the bear nipped the side of his neck, making him shiver.

"I have dessert for you, if you come sit with me," Peter said in his ear. One paw roamed down, and fingers trailed over his covered sheath. The fox gasped then and pressed back against the bear. The reflection in the glass showed him Peter was wearing an entirely different track suit, this one the color of blush wine.

Paws led him to a corner couch large enough for eight people, with a rolling cart from a hotel next to it with a wine bottle in a bucket and a covered platter. Peter took the large corner cushion and pulled the fox in close, kissing him on each ear and then the lips. Carson normally wasn't much of a fan of kissing, but the bear was very good at it, and then there was tongue, which made his sheath bulge in his pants.

"Where's Marshall?" The fox asked as he pulled back.

"He has apartment downstairs," the bear explained, one paw reaching around and popping open the button above Carson's tail. "He went until you want to go home." A few tugs and the fox's pants were shimmied down, leaving his emerging shaft still straining against his underwear. Carson went to pull down the bear's pants, and he lifted up enough to assist. However, unlike at his apartment, the fox pulled the bear's pants all the way down to his ankles. As before, he wasn't wearing underwear, and his cock was already extended a little from his sheath.

God, he smelled good. Carson could pick up hints of soap and pasta sauce in his fur, but his musk overpowered everything else. The fox slid down, pressing his lips against the emerging head of the bear's cock, running his tongue across it and watching as it completely stood to attention. He draped himself over the length of the couch, his tail in the air, one arm over Peter's belly, the other over his thighs, and pulled the bear's shaft in between his lips.

The bear was big, feeling bigger now that the fox had him in his muzzle, but manageable. When the head of his cock bumped the back of the fox's throat, he swallowed a few times until he heard a gasp as the bear went down his throat. Maybe this was the first time he'd been deep-throated, and Carson was glad he'd lost his gag reflex in college after multiple nights with that hot stallion. His nose pressed into thick fur, and he started sucking hard, clenching his throat around the invading member. He felt a paw slide down his back and into the back of his underwear, and he moaned around the cock as a large finger curved under his tail. He was wearing cute little black underwear that rode under his tail, which gave the bear more than enough room. One finger traced around his tailhole as he pulled up enough to taste precum, take a deep breath, and go back down again.

A paw came to rest on his head, and now when he pulled up for air, the bear gently guided him back down. The fox was in control, but the little insistence got him hard as hell in his briefs. The finger pulled away from his tailhole for a moment, and his ears swiveled when he heard something pop open. The smell of lube hit his nostrils only a second before a cool, slick finger started pressing back into his tailhole, and he needed to pull up to moan again. It pressed in deeper, and he knew the front of his briefs was ruined. When was the last time someone had done that? Normally when he blew someone, they just kept their paws on his shoulders or ears, but here was Peter, enjoying himself and teasing the fox just enough to motivate him. He wondered if the bear could go twice in one night, since he knew he wanted Peter's length under his tail.

A paw pushing down on the back of his head gave him only a second's warning before Peter held his breath. The fox pulled back, hearing the bear let out a sudden growl as he bobbed on the last few inches, swallowing as cum filled his muzzle. When he thought about it, the bear had held still when he came the last time, but Carson wanted to taste it now, as slutty as the idea sounded to him. He didn't lose a drop, even with the finger pushing further into him. Finally pulling off, he slurped the last few drops off, feeling the bear's hips jump from the sensitivity.

"You are even cuter like this," Peter said, wiggling his finger. Carson moaned, nuzzling against one of the bear's thighs. "You want me to take care of you, or you want to wait until I can go again?" He pulled his finger out, wiping the lube off on a towel hanging from the cart.

Why would someone expect him to answer questions when was he was painfully hard? His knot was already fully engorged, and he feared this pair of underwear would never get back into the right shape. However, resisting the urge to just quickly take care of himself, an idea popped into his head.

"Until you're ready," he said, putting that thought forward. His balls ached, and as he rolled over the feeling of his briefs rubbing against his trapped length wasn't helping anything, but he could wait.

The bear didn't bother pulling his pants back up. He reached over and pulled the cover off the waiting platter, and it took Carson a few seconds to realize what he was looking at. What was served on a bed of ice, still in tin cans? And then the smell hit his nostrils—fish eggs.

"Is that...caviar?" the fox asked.

"Not very expensive caviar, but yes," Peter said. "I figure, why not? Least I could do."

The least the bear could do was treat him to some burgers, but he wasn't in the mood to complain when he had an erection. Peter pulled the fox into his lap, reaching around him to carefully scoop a small amount of the black fish eggs onto a cracker and place it in front of the fox's lips. Carson blushed and ate it, feeling the small eggs burst against the roof of his mouth. He'd eaten roe at Japanese restaurants before, but this made that look like fast food. He closed his eyes, feeling himself getting a bit soft as he concentrated on the food.

When he tried to feed himself, the bear gently moved his paws away, kissing and nipping at the back of his neck. After a few tries, he gave up, letting Peter feed him caviar-covered crackers for a few minutes. It tasted good, too good for him, but there was something about being fed dessert in a naked bear's lap that just felt amazing. His cock was soft by the time Peter lifted a loaded cracker, gingerly placing the edge in between his teeth and tilting his muzzle at the fox. Carson took the hint and they kissed, the fox biting the cracker in half. After that last bite, a paw slid back down to his pre-soaked underwear, and he knew things were getting back on pace.

Peter stood up, walking the fox into the next room. It was a master bedroom with a king sized bed dominating the room, but the walls were even more impressive. Like the living room, it was a view to kill for, though this time of all the other big skyscrapers. If some pervert had a telescope, they could be watching this right now, and that got the fox harder faster. Why was he such an exhibitionist? Big fingers hooked into his underwear, pulling them and his pants

41

completely off. His shirt was unbuttoned right after, the bear's hard cock pressed against his rump.

"Take off your jacket," the fox said, and he felt the bear finish stripping, leaving them both naked in this exposed room. He pulled Peter to the bed, had him lie down on his back, and then Carson straddled his waist. The bear's length slid between his cheeks.

"Where's your lube?" he asked, and the bear reached over to pick up a small bottle on the bedside table. Carson recognized the brand—it was damn near twenty bucks for the tiny, fancy glass bottle. Peter reached behind the fox and slicked up his length, taking a second to rub the rest of the expensive lube on the fox's tailhole before pulling his paws back around to the fox's cock. However, Carson moved them to his hips. If the bear started stroking now, the fox would cum before he really got to enjoy this.

With a wiggle and a little guiding with one paw, the fox felt the tip of the bear's dripping length push into him. He was already a little stretched out, so after the head and first inch or so were inside him, the fox just leaned back, placing both paws on the bear's thighs and sinking down onto him. Peter let out a few approving noises, and Carson closed his eyes, feeling his length twitch once the bear was completely inside him.

No one ever let him ride them. It took forever to cum, and he was completely in charge even though he was on bottom. He could arch his back, wiggle, bounce, whatever he wanted, since the alternative for whoever was under him was not get to cum in a hot, athletic fox. Almost immediately he started letting out little gasps, squeezing around the member inside him, surprised the bear wasn't thrusting up into him or digging his blunt claws into his thighs. He seemed content to just let the fox do what he wanted, which was fine with Carson, since this was his favorite position.

Carson knew his own body very well, and knew how long he could go before instinct and carnal need overtook him just enjoying the act. It had been a very long time since he'd been in this position, and even longer than that since after a minute or two the person under him hadn't rolled them both over to pound him. The only time Peter moved was to slide paws down the fox's thighs, or give his length a stroke or two before Carson batted his paws away. He wanted to cum on his terms, and he was already close. His length practically screamed at him to finish himself off already, but he waited. He knew the bear couldn't last much longer. For some reason he couldn't really focus on, he wanted them to cum at the same time.

There it was—the tell. The bear clenched his teeth and held his breath. Carson felt the length inside him stiffen and start to pulse, so the fox wrapped one paw around his knot and squeezed hard, the other stroking his length fast. Right as he felt cum start to fill him, his first shot hit the bear across the belly. His toes curled—it was just what he wanted, clenching around the bear inside him, feeling the claws dug into his hips. It didn't really hurt, just accentuated the pleasure as he coated the bear with cum. Almost as fast it was over, and he slumped forward, the bear popping out of him with a wet sound and his muzzle pressed into the bear's shoulder as Carson panted hard. Big paws gripped his ass cheeks.

"You are…" the bear needed to catch his breath. "You are a kinky fox."

"That wasn't kinky," the fox replied, trying to breathe normally too. God, his ass was sore, but this was the most satisfied he'd been in a long time.

"I enjoy it too much," Peter said, "that makes it kinky."

It took them both a few minutes to recover, but once they did the bear led Carson into a shower large enough for three people to rinse off without touching each other and a dozen showerheads at all levels. However, there was no personal space between the two of them, since Peter soaped up the fox and Carson in return soaped up the bear. In the middle of rinsing off Peter got hard again, and when Carson shook his muzzle, he got to watch the bear jerk off, which was hot as hell. Peter might be a bit fat, but his arms and legs were all muscle, which showed even better with the bear's fur slicked down from the shower.

The dryers were a much more efficient model than the fox had, since his fur was dry within three minutes—he watched the bathroom clock, since he was curious—and then got to lie down on the couch as the bear brushed out his fur. Peter seemed to enjoy it, and Carson found it very soothing to have big, patient paws work down his back and tail. However, everything was over far too quickly, and soon he found himself pulling his pants back on, the bear opting to just keep a towel wrapped around his waist.

"I see you again soon?" the bear asked, buttoning up the fox's shirt and nibbling at his throat. If he wasn't careful, the fox would get hard again and have to spend the night. Now that his sex-and-incredible-apartment-fogged brain was easing out and his normal brain was shifting back into gear, he realized if he didn't leave now, he wouldn't want to. That kind of scared the crap out of him.

"I will text you," the fox said, making sure it was still in his control.

"Ok," Peter replied. "I am free all weekend."

This wasn't a date, he told the tiny voice in the back of his head. This was a hookup. A hookup who had served him caviar, but a hookup nonetheless. People who went on dates actually went out to places, in front of other people, and showed off. That wasn't this. Peter had showed off his apartment to make the sex more intense, he reasoned. He'd been impressed, the same way he was impressed when that wolf investment baker always showed up in a thousand-dollar suit. Of course, that wolf didn't kiss him. Dammit, this was probably something more. Carson didn't want something more. Or did he?

He pushed the thought out of his head as Peter called Marshall back up to the apartment. Before the terrier arrived, Peter lifted the bottle of wine out of the bucket, wiped it off with a towel from the kitchen, and placed it in a paper bag, probably from whatever store Marshall had purchased it.

"You drink it with your friends," Peter said, passing the bag to him. Well, Carson thought, the bottle might impress Richard.

"Thanks," he said, accepting a last kiss from the bear before the elevator doors opened. Marshall didn't get out, and waited for the fox to step in before he closed the doors.

"Will you need to make any stops on the way home?" The bull terrier asked. He was still wearing a suit with tails, the fox noticed, but it was a different tie, this one a dark blue.

"No," he said. Judging by when he'd been using the dryers in the bathroom, it was barely after midnight. The thought of a limo dropping him off at a bar or something else that would still be open bothered him.

They rode in silence for most of the trip, with the fox occasionally shifting his sitting position in the back of the limo because of his sore backside. To Marshall's credit, he didn't say a word, even though the fox bet the butler knew exactly what had gone down. He checked his phone, and like every Saturday night, he had a few dozen messages. His cock wasn't into it right now, so he quietly deleted messages and saved the hotter profiles to look at later. What was the harm? Peter was on here too, and looking at the public messages left on the bear's profile, he wouldn't be lonely unless he wanted to be. 'Other Info: Russian Accent' on Peter's page definitely wasn't hurting matters. He got so engrossed reading the comments on Peter's page that he didn't notice they'd stopped until the door opened beside him.

"I hope to see you again soon," the bull terrier said as Carson got out and pocketed his phone.

"Me too," he said automatically, but then thought about it. "I mean, I appreciate you driving me…all the way back out here." Fuck, he was bad at all this interpersonal stuff when he wasn't at work.

"Not a problem, sir," Marshall said.

Carson just nodded and walked into his apartment building. He could hear a few parties, and he felt his phone vibrate when he walked past one door, indicating someone was active on Knotz in that apartment. It might be that Rottweiler, but he didn't care to check right now.

Once he got to his own apartment, he unlocked the door, stepped in, bolted it behind him, and just started stripping. All of his clothes smelled like bear, and right now, he just felt like sleeping without smelling like someone else. He set the bag with the wine bottle in it on the couch to deal with tomorrow. Naked, he flopped into bed, the nagging thought that he'd just been on a date popping back into his head a few moments before he fell asleep.

# Chapter Four: ChrisKitty

When Carson woke up, he really wanted to get Peter out of his mind. He had really bad morning wood, thanks to a dream of getting fucked in that amazing shower, but consciously the fox didn't want to dwell. Did he have to work today? After rolling out of bed, he checked the schedule on the fridge: in about an hour. Well, he could get a palate cleanser during lunch, or after work. There was nothing quite like fucking someone else to get the image of the first person out of his head. His ass was still sore, but it was a pleasant soreness, since it reminded him of the pleasure, not the conflicting emotions. He'd need to top someone, since he wasn't up for getting rammed again so soon.

He pulled his phone out of his discarded pants and flipped through messages. His mom had sent him some pictures of her garden, specifically the new tomato plants. Mom might like junk food like everyone else, but she tended to grow anything that could fit on her patio. He was right about most of last night's messages—that Rottweiler must live downstairs. He wasn't online right now, so the fox couldn't check. Also, there was a text message from his boss.

*Richard was able to take Sarah's days. You don't have to come in today.*

Well, there went his entire plan for today. Hooking up early in the day was rare, unless he got lucky with a search on Knotz, so for now, he decided against it. Finding someone cute right now was like going to a strip club on a Tuesday—the odds were you'd be disappointed.

He turned on the news and decided to do some laundry. It wasn't glamorous, but if he wanted to look half-decent tonight—even if his clothes were only going to stay on for a few minutes—it would be worth it. His phone buzzed every now and then while he organized the apartment, but he ignored it until he finished.

When the station switched from important happenings around the world to game shows, the fox curled up on the couch with a soda and flipped through messages. There was a way-too-skinny wolf who wanted to fuck, but he preferred his wolves muscular, so he deleted that message. That black cat he'd marked as interesting had posted a few more pictures, but just like before, everything stayed a bit classy. If he was free tonight, Carson felt he'd have a good time.

When he looked over, he realized the paper bag with the wine in it was still sitting against one of the arms of the couch. He kept his apartment rather cold, so it wasn't like it could go bad. He pulled the bottle out of the bag, and looking through the clear glass, he realized it was champagne. That matched the fancy evening of caviar and the wonderful apartment. He placed it in his fridge. Maybe he'd share it with his mom.

A few minutes later a picture came through on his phone. Carson licked his lips—Peter had sent him something good. The bear was balls-deep in a wolf, the canine's strong back taking up most of the shot. The other guy might not have even known the bear was getting evidence, which to him made it hotter. The second picture was after Peter had cum all over the wolf's back.

Rather than just sit around and look at cock pictures for the rest of the day, the fox decided to get some more stuff done. His fridge was nearly empty, but since he didn't own a car, he could only buy what would fit in his backpack. He found his bag crumpled in the back of his closet and figured that was the best use of his time right now.

One of the distinct disadvantages of living in such a large city was the lack of a supermarket. Sure, there were three or four grocery stores within a reasonable distance, but nothing gigantic like out in the country. The one closest was the main food source for everyone in Papillon, and the decorations showed they enjoyed the business. As Carson walked through the automated doors, rainbow flags poked out from each wall. Somehow the grocery store was warmer than his apartment. That did not bode well for the life expectancy of his air conditioning.

Cute guys abounded here too, but in the middle of the day, it was more the 'househusband' variety. A handsome wolf pushed a cart with a toddler in the front; a rabbit had a horde of children of various heights surrounding him. Carson didn't really understand that—there was always the joke that rabbits had a lot of kids, but when you had to adopt, he'd thought it wouldn't stand up. However, here was a gay rabbit with eight children of different fur colors and ages. Maybe he was a foster parent. Carson couldn't see himself doing that either. He just didn't see himself as nurturing.

"Hey, Carson," someone said as he loaded a basket with peppers. It was a fennec fox, dressed gayer than even Carson could manage.

48

The rainbow ear piercings were just a little too much. The red fox thought he recognized him, but he wasn't sure.

"It's Mikhail. From college."

"Oh, right," Carson said. They hugged, but it took him a minute to remember how close they'd gotten. He'd never hooked up with the fennec, but he remembered seeing him at the occasional frat party. They might have made out while drunk, but that didn't really count.

"When did you move here?" Carson asked. Achaia University was halfway across the country.

"About six months ago," Mikhail answered, picking up his own vegetables while they walked past the trays. "I got a job with Crementi Designs, so my boyfriend and I decided it would be fun to live up here."

"Where's he working then?" Carson asked. Dammit, he really wasn't good at small talk. He looked away, pretending to inspect the tomatoes while he grasped for something else to talk about after this topic ran its course. Mikhail was cute, but Carson had a very strict 'no cheating' policy. If the fennec broke up with his boyfriend and wanted a rebound, that was fine, but he would not be the cock that split them up.

"He got hired by the Bookkeepers down on 34th street. He's the store manager."

Carson actually dropped the tomato in his paw, which gave him time to recover as he retrieved it. How was Terrence gay? How had he not known? The proper, well-dressed lion gave no indication of it at all, and Carson generally found he had weapons-grade gaydar. By the time he placed the fruit in his basket, he was able to hold his tongue. Mikhail didn't seem to notice.

"Who're you dating then? I bet he's cute," the fennec said with a grin.

What could he answer to that? Here was someone who'd graduated the same time as him, and already settled down in a nice neighborhood with a nice job. He'd bet good money that the fennec lived in a townhouse or something else way above Carson's pay grade. Since this conversation could go on longer if he didn't give an answer, his panicked mind brought out the first answer that came to mind.

"He's a bear," Carson said quickly, ducking into the bread aisle.

Mikhail, however, was quick on the beat, and stuck his tongue out at the other fox. "Oohhh, see, I always thought you liked little twinky guys," Mikhail said.

"I do," Carson said, though that was only partially true. He liked skinny guys who were, in his mind, 'supposed' to be skinny, like small cats and mustelids. If it was a wolf or bull, he expected them to be muscular if they wanted to fuck him. Now that he thought about it, the only non-twink Mikhail had probably seen him with was Roberto, who had been a skinny horse, just muscular-skinny.

"So, what?" Mikhail asked, picking up some bagels. "Is he hung?"

"Pretty well," Carson said, showing size with his paws. Now here was a topic Carson could add details to. If someone asked him about his emotions, he was bound to freeze, but cock he could discuss all day.

"Terrence is too," the fennec said, blushing a little around his ears. "Though he'd kill me for telling other people." The fennec's huge ears flicking was cute, but Carson pushed the thought aside. There would never be any sex with Mikhail. That ship had sailed.

"How is he in bed?" Carson asked. "I've never had good luck with big cats." Knowing this much about his boss might otherwise be uncomfortable, but he considered Mikhail a college friend. Besides, if Terrence wanted to put him in charge of returns again, he could always ask him how Mikhail was doing. He didn't really see the point of being friends with your boss, but the concept of it definitely couldn't hurt.

"Oh, y'know..." Mikhail said as they moved into the soda section. He noticed Mikhail still drank those really fruity off-brand things. Carson only bought them to mix with vodka. "...as long as you know about the claws and teeth before, it's really fun."

"So, he likes it rough then?" Carson asked. Mikhail's smile was infectious.

"Nope," the fennec said, putting a six-pack of Strawberry Xplosion in his cart. "According to him, he's not rough for a lion, since he doesn't leave marks. He told me about a guy from his college who always left really deep scratches."

"Eww," they both said, and Carson smiled. He now had a distinct urge to play with that black cat tonight.

"You should come over and have drinks with us some time," Mikhail said as they made it to the registers.

"I don't think that's such a good idea," Carson said. His basket was a lot healthier than Mikhail's—he wondered how the fennec stayed so skinny.

"Why not? It's not like we'll want to have a freaky threesome or something," Mikhail said. From the look on the Dalmatian cashier's face, he'd be up for one.

"It's not that," Carson said. "Terrence is my boss."

Now, Mikhail seemed surprised, though he wasn't as good at hiding it. "Are you the one that's always on his phone, or the slutty one who's always flirting with customers?"

"On my phone," Carson said. "The slutty one is Mark." Terrence was apparently not aware of Knotz. Good. That meant his boss just thought he surfed the web or texted, rather than planned to get cock on lunch breaks. Mark openly flirted with every cute fox or dog that came into the store. He was their evening barista, and took home a lot of tips, and presumably a lot of guys, though Carson had never gone home with him. He smelled too sharply like coffee grounds.

They both finished checking out, and when they were on the sidewalk, Mikhail pulled out his phone and showed Carson the number. The red fox typed it into his own, glad he'd closed Knotz before walking over here.

"If you want to hang out this weekend, just text me," the fennec said. "Bring the bear if you want to." He winked before starting to sashay over to a sports car parked at the meter. He definitely had some money. Did fashion designers really make that much? Also, come to think of it, he hadn't told Mikhail his supposed boyfriend's name. Dammit, he didn't want to think of Peter as his boyfriend. He was just a bear he liked hooking up with. Then again, no one else had ever bought him caviar.

His phone buzzed with a bank alert. His paycheck had been deposited, and apparently the bookstore had done quite well, since he'd received a few hundred dollars more than expected. Now it was time to set up with Richard. He'd need practice before trying to socialize with Terrence outside of work and Mikhail without weed.

*Want to look at phones tonight?* He texted the coyote. It took a few minutes for him to respond.

*Sure. Can you get some rum?* Richard sent back to him.

They could have a couple of rum and cokes, talk about books, and Carson could ease into the idea of socializing with his pants on and without a cell phone. If he got horny, he would wait until after the coyote left his apartment. Richard probably had a bunch of questions about authors and the like, since tastes in this area were pretty broad.

He put his groceries away, eyeing the bottle of champagne that was still in his fridge. He could write that off as part of his bonus check, and he knew Richard would appreciate trying it. It was probably an expensive brand, since it had come with caviar, and by his earlier conversation with Richard, he'd probably never tried anything higher-end. He checked the label, but it was in French. In his opinion, that confirmed its price.

There was a liquor store that delivered, so he ordered two bottles of rum, one nice and one cheap, one of those rapper-endorsed fruity vodkas that tasted like liquid gay, and two six-packs of beer in case they wanted to take it a little slow. He wasn't a wine fan, but ordered a bottle anyway for when he visited Mikhail and Terrence. Nothing like a peace offering to stop the lion from talking about work.

It took an hour for the store to deliver, so he went to cleaning his apartment. It was never what he would consider 'dirty', but there was definitely fur on every surface outside the kitchen, and a lot of it didn't belong to him. He turned on all the ceiling fans, since the scent of sex still clung to a few surfaces, and de-scented everything he could. Even if he wasn't going to fuck Richard, he still changed the sheets in case someone new came over after, and washed the old sheets just so the scent wasn't in his bedroom. The bathroom needed a lot of work as well.

His intercom buzzed, and he went down to pick up his booze. As the ram passed him the cardboard box, he felt his own phone buzz and heard the ram's do the same thing. He looked the delivery guy up and down. Well, Carson definitely recognized parts of him. To his credit, the ram chuckled.

"Looks like I'll need to deliver here more often," the ram said. The name CHARLIE was embroidered on his shirt. No wonder he had such a nice ass, if he was lifting boxes of liquor all day.

"Not tonight," the fox said, signing the receipt. "But definitely soon." He watched the ram get back on his scooter, thankful for the view. The black cat was still on his mind, though the ram vied for an opening in the next few days.

Carson just watched television for the next few hours, flipping through channels and overall doing nothing. He found the 'old paper' air scent that sprayed every few minutes his mom has bought him, which made his apartment smell like a library. Nothing much happened on Sunday, apparently, so the evening news was filled with the normal political stuff and stories of talented puppies who sounded like they could talk like people. He never understood why those were on the news.

Richard arrived a few minutes after seven, with a laptop bag and a very severe blush. He hadn't changed out of his polo shirt from work. Carson wondered why, and came to a conclusion almost immediately.

"This isn't a date," the fox said. Immediately, the coyote relaxed.

"Oh, ok," Richard said. "I didn't think it was." Bullshit, the fox thought, but he didn't bring it up. If the coyote was this nervous about the *idea* of a date, Carson wouldn't ask if he was dating anyone.

The coyote set up his laptop on the fox's dining room table while Carson poured drinks. Since he wasn't sure how much Richard drunk, he made the first rum and coke weak. When his coworker sipped it without a problem, the fox decided to make the next round a bit stronger. If Richard was poor enough to not own a real cell phone, he'd probably taken the bus over or walked.

"Ok…" the coyote said. "What about these?" Richard had pulled up a page of cell phones.

"All of those aren't including the activation fees and plans," Carson said. He leaned over the coyote to change the page. His scent was light, and the fox realized he hadn't been able to pick it up while at work. He pushed those thoughts down. Richard was not here to hook up. He was here as a friend.

"Take a look at these," Carson said. "You'll need to pick it up in-store, but don't let them talk you into a long plan. It'll be a little more expensive monthly, but none of the more bullshit fees."

Richard nodded while the fox took a long swig from his rum and coke. This grown-up socializing was remarkably more stressful than he had considered. Maybe he'd need some female friends, just so his body didn't try to respond when they were close by. He'd been so conditioned that having a guy in his apartment meant sucking dick that his body just assumed everyone nearby wanted to be part of all that. In the last few years it wasn't wrong, but it was time the fox try to reprogram, at least partially.

"I like this one," the coyote eventually said while the fox poured himself a second drink. "It looks neat, and I can get apps on it."

"The store on the corner probably has that one," Carson said.

"Mind if I run down and pick it up?" Richard said. "I don't know how to program it."

"You don't program a smartphone," the fox said, and then realized what the coyote was talking about. "Oh, you want to know how to download stuff on it."

"Yeah," Richard said. He'd only been sipping his drink, and it wasn't even halfway finished.

"Sure, I'll help," Carson said, picking up his coworker's glass. "I'll pop this in the fridge."

"Thanks," he said. "I'll be right back."

It only took Richard about twenty minutes to make the round-trip from the cell phone shop back to the fox's apartment. They plugged the phone into the coyote's laptop so it would charge, then got it to connect to Carson's wi-fi.

"Ok, what do you want me to install?" the fox asked.

"Uh…" Richard blushed. "How about Bookkeeper's app?"

"Sure," the fox said, thumbing through the app store. Judging by just how red the coyote's ears were getting, he wanted much more intimate stuff on here. His tail wagged while Carson showed him how to go through the store as the app downloaded.

"Here," he said, passing the phone back to its owner. "Hold down the mic and say a title."

"Uhhh…" Richard froze.

"Try something you've rung up recently," Carson offered. He made another drink while the coyote thought it through.

"*Legacy*," he said, and when the app didn't immediately respond, he added, "by President Forks." Now the app showed a book with its page turning as a loading screen, then popped up with a message: 'Did you mean Albert Forks?'

"Yes," Carson said over his shoulder. The app moved again, and the book popped up.

"That was easy," Richard mumbled. He pressed the button again. "Local pickup." This time, a map popped up with the bookstores in town that still had it in stock.

"Can I use this at work?" he asked.

"It's generally more accurate than the computers," the fox answered. He passed the coyote back his drink. He took a swig this time.

"So this is how I do every app?" Richard asked.

"Yup," the fox said, turning back to refill his own glass. When he walked around to turn on his television, he peeked at the smartphone. Now the coyote was focused on the 'social' section, particularly the dating apps.

"Most of them are paid," Carson said, and Richard nearly jumped out of his fur.

"You want gay or straight ones?" he asked. The fox thought steam was about to come out of the coyote's ears. "You're in Papillon. No one cares."

Carson had never seen someone's eyes glaze over before, so he watched in mild fascination while the coyote reacted to the new information. It must have never occurred to the poor kid that living in a gay district meant that he could just do whatever—and whoever—he wanted, and judgment for that was a thing that happened elsewhere. It would be much more likely someone here would criticize his clothes than whoever he was kissing on the street.

"Gay," the coyote whispered, his ears down. Not entirely sure what to do, the fox put an arm around his shoulders and gave him a friendly nuzzle.

"Don't worry about it. Half your coworkers are," he whispered. Richard stiffened.

"You?"

"Yup."

"Michael?"

"Nope. Three kids."

"Mark?"

"Bi." Now there was a pause.

"Terrence?"

"Him too."

Richard's eyes went wide. While he adjusted to the whole new universe around him, Carson refilled his drink, making this one a double. The coyote drained it.

"I mean, I knew there were a lot of gay people here when I moved here, but…really? That many?" he mumbled. The coyote sat down on the couch, looking dazed, setting his phone down beside him.

"You're in the largest gay district in the country," Carson said. This was turning into an interesting evening. "You knew that, right?" He gave Richard his third drink. This time, he took a big gulp, and then started to sip it.

"I mean, I knew it was safe, but I didn't expect…" he waved his free paw. "This."

"The rainbow flags and the naked guys walking down the street when it's hot out?" the fox offered.

"Yeah," Richard muttered. "That."

"You get used to it after a while," Carson said, taking a seat next to him. "You don't even notice the weirder things after a year or two."

"How long have you lived here?" the coyote asked.

"Forever," he said, sticking out his tongue. "My mom lives a few blocks up. Just went away for college, then came back." Carson turned on the streaming video player.

"I'll turn on some stand-up while you look through apps," he said, while the coyote went back to looking at his phone.

Through a few sideways glances, the fox observed that Richard was mainly looking for what would be considered 'normal' dating apps, but they were all pricey or came with monthly fees. He went through page after page, trying to find a free one.

"None of the ones with compatibility are going to be free," Carson said. "The only free ones are hookup apps." The fox rolled a finger over the screen a few pages until it showed Knotz and its competitors.

"Knotz is for gay sex, The Howling is just Canids, Purr is all cats, Hibernite is for bears…" He ticked off the whole page. He'd tried nearly all of them before settling on Knotz. Richard just nodded as he explained.

"Download whichever ones you want. Most of them have a 'premium' version. Knotz is no ads if you pay ten bucks."

"Oh, ok," the coyote said.

"Can I make the profile on my computer?" Richard asked a few minutes later. "I'm not good at typing on this yet."

Carson could guess which app he was talking about. "No, but you'll get used to it," the fox said. "Just make sure your phone's sound is off at work. Knotz is really loud."

Richard blushed all over again, but the fox pretended not to notice. His phone buzzed. It was a picture of Peter getting head from a rabbit. Carson closed it very quickly, but apparently not fast enough.

"You have very…open friends," the coyote mumbled.

"You could say that," Carson said, his turn to blush. He really needed to get laid tonight, but a coworker was not the way to go. Dammit, he needed to try not to get hard now while Richard was in the apartment. The rum helped a little with that, and he could save the champagne for another day.

"How about you come by again later this week?" Carson said. "I can get you used to the scene."

"What scene?" the coyote asked. This was going to be a bit more complicated than the fox had thought.

"The gay scene. We could go to a club, or a bar." It took Richard almost a full ten seconds to answer.

"That sounds…really nice."


After the comedy special was over, the coyote gave him a very tight hug, then left in a hurry. He probably wanted to go through all the cock on his new phone in a privacy of his own apartment, which the fox completely understood. In the last twenty minutes, Peter had sent him a few more pictures of him and the bunny, the last with the rabbit's face covered in cum. The fox needed a hookup, and he needed it now.

There was a feature he tended not to use on Knotz—the 'get direct' button. It sent an alert to whoever he indicated, whether that be one person or a group, that he wanted to get laid right now. No conversation, no flirting via text: just someone arriving within a matter of minutes, ready to have fun. He did just that for the cute black cat. The app confirmed he was on his way a minute later.

Carson let the black cat walk right up, and met him at the front door. He was very cute, and if the fox was in a more romantic mood, he would be someone to spend a few hours with, trying all sorts of positions, but right now, he just wanted to get hard and get off. The feline didn't say a word, just smiled when the fox shut the door behind him.

They undressed each other, since even if the fox was already hard in his underwear, he wanted to explore the cat's body. He was thin, but not too thin, and under his shirt had both his nipples and his belly button pierced. Carson kneeled to lightly tug on one of the nipple rings with his teeth, and the cat let out a gasp. He kept all his kinkier secrets under his clothes, since when the fox helped the cat step out of his shorts, he found a small silver bar through the base of his sheath. His cock was already escaping, so the fox swirled his tongue around the exposed head. The cat hadn't posted a single cock pic, and the fox would have messaged him sooner if he knew about the piercings. Carson had always liked piercings, but never had the stomach to get them himself.

Paws gripped his ears, sharp claws pricking at the skin as he started to bob his head. He undid his pants, letting his hard cock into the air, idly stroking himself with one paw, though he didn't plan to spurt on his own carpet. The cat started to rock his hips, shifting his weight between his toes and heels while the fox played with the piercing with his tongue. He felt the cat shudder, and didn't stop sucking as the first load sprayed into his muzzle. Cats could always go a few times, and even if the black cat didn't say anything, the taste on his tongue told the fox he enjoyed it.

Carson stood back up, gripped one of the cat's wrists, and led him into the bedroom. He purred very loudly, so the fox figured he was up for anything. After getting the cat on the bed—he immediately rolled into his knees, head resting on his arms, his tail lashing in the air—the fox pulled out his lube. As much fun as it would be to just slam into the other guy, he wasn't in the mood for total control. He pulled off his own shirt and kicked his pants into the corner before climbing on the bed.

The cat didn't complain when Carson rolled him onto his side. They were spooning, and the fox thought it might be cute if he wasn't rubbing lube on his cock. He reached around, grabbing the black cat's re-hardening cock as he pushed into his tailhole. The other guy was still purring up a storm, and when the fox bottomed out, his knot pressed firmly against flesh, the cat squeezed down around him, nuzzling back against the fox. Carson wrapped his other arm around the smaller guy's shoulders and started thrusting.

He wouldn't last long, even if it had been less than a day since the last time he came. However, he wanted to tie, so already being in a comfortable position was always a good idea. He thrust into the small cat, listening to his sharp breathing and purring. This was the life. No commitments, no worries.

His knot popped in and the cat hissed, but almost immediately afterward came in the fox's paw. Carson gave him a few more thrusts before he bit down on the back of the cat's neck and filled him. God, it felt good to cum in someone. Maybe he could turn the tables and top Peter next time they got together.

Dammit, he didn't want to think about the bear when he was balls-deep inside a cute cat. The other guy started wiggling, so the fox stopped stroking. The black cat started to try and pull away, so Carson gripped him a little harder.

"I'm tied," he said, wincing at the pressure from each tug. However, the cat rolled over onto his belly, the fox's weight on top of him, and the cat's paws started to rummage under the pillows. Awkwardly because of their position, Carson tried to help, and his paw closed around something small, hard and plastic.

"This?" he asked, holding it in front of the cat's nose. Carson didn't know what it was, but his question was immediately answered when the cat pushed it into one ear and wiggled. Then, a second question entered his mind, one he couldn't block before it reached his lips.

"Is that why you use Knotz?" The cat clenched around him, making him wince. Apparently that was not a question he should have asked.

Once they could pull apart, the cat cleaned up, then left without a word. However, questions still bubbled in Carson's mind. Why did he care why the cat used the hookup app? Was that any of his business?

Why did he use Knotz in the first place? That answer was shamefully simple, when he sat still for a few seconds and just thought about it. He didn't need to know social cues, he didn't need to get to know someone, and he didn't have to ever call them back or awkwardly break up if things didn't work out. It was just the one aspect of a relationship, without any of the bullshit.

Was that necessarily good, though? He didn't know much about Peter—who just kept popping up in his mind, despite what he thought he wanted—but they got along well, even when their pants were still on. Maybe he'd try a date. He could go a few days without a cock in his ass, anyway. It would make the next time 'special', if he could call a few days between hookups special.

# Chapter Five: <No Such User Exists>

*Want to see a movie with me?* Peter's text read.

It had been a few days since the last time he'd gotten a message from the bear, and that had been a picture of a white fox in his lap. Carson had abstained from Knotz for most of the last few days, trying to think about the idea of 'dating' as a concept. Today had been when he decided to hook up again, and if this didn't work, he still had nothing else to do for a few hours until he'd planned to go by Mikhail and Terrence's apartment. Then, fucking. He'd only worked the morning today, and wanted something a bit off-the-wall for tonight. Maybe a sun bear or a rat would be fun. Or Peter, which he knew would turn out well.

*Shouldn't you be at work? :-P* He sent back. He assumed the bear worked all day.

*Computers are being switched out at office. We had to take a vacation day.* That made sense. However, the real question was, did the fox want to go someplace with the bear where they had to stay fully dressed? He was nice company, in that the bear didn't chatter. He didn't respond until he'd made it back to his apartment and put his groceries away. It couldn't hurt, he told himself, and if he decided to hang out with Mikhail, he definitely didn't want to go alone under the glare of his boss. A test run with Peter in a 'normal' situation might be worth it. Even if he wanted to get the bear out of his head. Well, he just didn't want to fantasize too much. If they were fuck-buddies, that was fine.

*I get to pick the movie.* Carson texted back. Knotz flashed. He ignored it.

*No problem. I will be there in half an hour. Is that alright?* Came the response.

*Sure.* Carson sent back.

About forty minutes later, Carson heard his intercom buzz. He grabbed a hoodie from his closet, since it looked like it was going to rain, and turned his phone off—the closest theater still got pissy if a phone buzzed. He tensed when he saw the limousine. Peter was standing outside at the back door, rather than Marshall, and dressed in a well-tailored gray suit.

"I thought we were just going to the movies," Carson asked, carefully keeping his eyes off passerby.

"Yes," Peter answered. "Marshall was in middle of errands, so he will drop us off."

"Can he drop us off…a little further away?" Carson asked.

Peter chuckled as he led the fox into the back of the limo, shutting the door behind him. The bear pressed close, kissing Carson on the cheek before they started moving. A paw also grabbed his sheath. Both moved away quickly, but it didn't stop the fox from having to pull his hoodie down a little.

"What movie you want to see?" Peter said, and when the fox noticed the front seat/back seat window was closed, he calmed down a little. Marshall might know they were fucking, but he didn't want the British dog to see it.

"The new fantasy movie that came out," the fox said. "Dragonhunt."

"Sounds fun," Peter said. "I like those kind of movies." The bear put an arm around his shoulders, and Carson absentmindedly leaned against him. Whatever his suit was made out of was really soft.

"Why no tracksuit this time?" the fox asked.

"I am not allowed to wear them at work," the bear said, his fingers rubbing one of the fox's ears. That was way too relaxing for its own good. "I wear them all other time. Very comfortable."

"I feel I'm underdressed," Carson mumbled, and the bear leaned over to nibble at his other ear. The fox was now trying very much not to get hard right now.

"Here," he whispered, before detaching for a few seconds to wiggle out of his coat and drape his tie over one of the armrests. His shirt was gray and fitted tight against his arms and belly. Carson needed to breathe evenly to calm down. They weren't going to fuck in the theater, though the fox suspected his plans for the rest of the day might be derailed. Why did he react like this every time around the bear? Sure, he was damn near constantly horny, but he hadn't started getting hard around Mikhail, even if he found him really cute. What made Peter so special?

Marshall dropped them off a block from the theater, and as they walked, the bear reached over and held his paw. He smiled, and Carson couldn't help but smile back. Is this what a date was like? He hadn't really 'gone out' with anyone since high school, and then it had been girls. In college, once he'd figured out he liked cock, there had been a lot of it, and not a lot of pretense.

Peter bought the tickets and walked him in, the fox still quietly in his own thoughts. It took him until they were waiting in line for popcorn for the fox to realize he was being shy. Him, shy? What did he have to be shy about? He'd met hookups naked and hard at the door, but a bear holding his paw made him nervous.

Maybe this was different, though, he thought. This took a lot more multitasking to do. Sex was just physics. This is chemistry, and hormones, and smells, and little touches, and all that other stuff. If he really didn't want to be here, he wouldn't have answered the text. Besides, what did one date hurt? If they didn't do anything afterwards, he'd call up that hot Rottweiler. Hell, even if they did do something after this, it wasn't like Knotz was going anywhere.

They found two seats in the middle of the theater, the bear's arm draping back over his shoulder once they settled in. This wasn't bad, the fox thought. He was comfortable, he'd wanted to see this anyway, and having the bear next to him was oddly soothing. He placed a paw on the bear's knee, and heard a grunt of approval.

*Dragonhunt* turned out to be incredibly shitty. Some of the actors were hot, but the effects looked ten years old and Carson kept laughing when he wasn't supposed to. Peter chuckled at times as well, so he figured they'd both ended up having a good time. The popcorn bucket stayed in the bear's lap, which gave the fox more than enough opportunities to reach over and give him an occasional grope with one paw while he ate. The bear definitely didn't mind that.

The theater lobby was much more crowded when they left, and Carson realized it must be late enough for school to be out. They made their way through the crowd, and once they were out on the sidewalk, the bear took his paw.

"What happens now?" the fox asked.

"We can go to dinner," Peter said. Carson had an idea.

"Want to stop by one of my friends?" he asked. "They invited me over tonight."

"Should we bring wine?" the bear asked.

"I still have that champagne," Carson said. "I think that'll do."

"Ah," Peter said, and there was a pause. "Why have you not drunk it?"

63

"Wasn't an occasion," Carson said as they waited at a crosswalk.

"Your friend will like it. It is expensive," the bear said. The fox didn't really consider that a sign of good taste, since he'd had foie gras once and thought it was gross.

Marshall picked them up at a corner, and they drove back to the fox's apartment. After just a few gropes—the fox didn't want to go to Mikhail's house smelling entirely of sex—he texted the fennec.

*Are we still on for tonight?* He asked. It only took a few minutes to get a response, most of which the fox spent in the bear's lap. It was comfortable there.

*Yup. Are you allergic to anything? I'm cooking :).* The fennec sent back.

"You have any allergies?" He asked the bear.

"No," Peter said. That was officially more than he knew about everyone else he'd slept with. Maybe the bear was his boyfriend, after all. He tried not to focus on the idea right now.

"Ok, they are cooking. Should I ask if champagne goes with what they're making?" he asked. The bear shrugged.

"Champagne is always good."

It didn't take them long to be driven to Mikhail's house. The fennec had texted him the address, and like he expected, the two had a much swankier place than the red fox. They lived in a townhouse on the line between Papillon and downtown, surrounded by the best shops and convenient to everywhere in the city. Apparently Carson should have majored in something other than American Literature. They rang the doorbell, and Terrence met them at the door. Unlike at work, where he always wore a pressed shirt and tie, now the lion was in a St. Marx Strikers jersey. Carson would not have pegged him as a basketball fan.

"Hey," the lion said, and to the fox's surprise, he noticed the big cat's ears flicking every which way and his tail lashing; he was embarrassed. He must not have wanted coworkers to know he was gay.

"We brought this," Peter said, breaking the awkward silence. "I hope you like." The bear passed over the bottle.

Terrence glanced at the label as he stepped aside to let them into his home. Carson really liked the interior design, but since he figured that was Mikhail's job, it made sense everything looked nice. The walls, rather than the off-white of his apartment, had been painted a dark red, which gave the admittedly small space a very comfy feel, almost like a log cabin. The furniture was all big and plush, even with a few stuffed animals placed here and there. The art made Carson smirk—the walls were all covered in framed posters of old-fashioned pinup models. Mikhail definitely didn't like girls, but must like the aesthetic. Did Terrence? Was it weird to ask if he was bisexual? This whole 'making friends as an adult' thing was difficult.

"Sweetie, where'd you put the cumin?" Mikhail called out. Terrence's mane practically stood out on end as he rushed to the kitchen. Carson decided to just admire the posters so the lion couldn't see him trying to suppress a giggle. There were a lot of affectionate words he could understand attributed to Terrence, but 'sweetie' definitely wasn't one of them.

"He does not seem to like us in the house," Peter whispered in his ear. One of his big arms slid around his shoulders, pulling him close enough so the bear could kiss one of his ears.

"I think he's not used to people knowing he's gay," Carson whispered back. "I didn't know he was until a few days ago."

"He lives here. This city is very gay," the bear countered, but the fox just shook his head.

"Not the same thing. He's…" he groped for the right thing to say, especially since there was kind of a language barrier. "…not all gay about his gayness? Like you. I wouldn't have known."

"I do not care if people know," the bear said, nuzzling his shoulder. Why was he suddenly so affectionate? The fox didn't really mind, but it couldn't lead to anything right now.

"Some people still think it's not anybody else's business," the fox said.

Mikhail stepped out of the kitchen then, which made Carson unable to suppress his giggle any longer. The fennec still had those rainbow earrings in, but now also wore an apron embroidered with the words 'BLOW THE CHEF' and covered in glittery trumpets. Peter snorted, trying to cover up the noise with one paw.

"I hope you guys like curry," the fennec said. "Want me to put the chilies in it?"

"Sure," Carson and Peter both said. They looked at each other. The fox couldn't help but smile a little more. He'd told Mikhail they were dating. It couldn't hurt anything. Anyway, he was still fucking other people and so was the bear. This wasn't anything serious.

"Do you guys...want to watch the game?" the lion asked. Carson didn't even know what sports were on which days, so he went out on a conversational limb.

"Who are the Strikers playing?" the fox asked. Apparently that was the correct question, since Terrence relaxed a little.

"Founders," he said and turned on the TV. Carson squinted to read the corner of the screen. Apparently they were from Washington, D.C.

"I do not understand this game," Peter said, taking a seat on the couch next to Terrence. "Why was that throw worth more than the other one?"

While Terrence explained how basketball worked to Peter, Carson escaped to the kitchen. He knew how the game worked—he just didn't care. If he wanted to watch sweaty guys handle balls for a few hours, he had the Internet for that.

"Need any help in here?" he asked as he stepped around the corner. Carson had never been a very good cook besides the basics of bachelorhood, but he knew a professional kitchen when he saw one. Mikhail might as well have television cameras set up to show housewives how to bake.

"I'm good," the fennec fox said. He stood in front of the stove, a large cauldron of something that looked like gumbo bubbling in front of him. He stirred it every few seconds, and it definitely smelled delicious. Carson also noticed a rice cooker steaming a few feet away.

"What...is it?" he asked.

"Beef curry," the fennec said, his tail swishing back and forth. "Do you like the place? We just rented it about a month ago."

"Lot nicer than my apartment," Carson said. "How can you afford this place?"

"Crementi Designs. They pay me to tell rich people how to decorate their houses. Terrence makes pretty good money too."

"Wait...you make more than Terrence does?" Carson had a vague idea of how much his boss made from peeking at normal manager rates.

"About five times as much," Mikhail whispered. "It's *stupid* how much I make doing this." Well, the red fox had definitely picked the wrong career.

"What does Peter do?" the fennec fox asked.

"Hedge fund manager," he answered.

"Ooo. Sounds like he's crazy rich."

Carson frowned, but the fennec just started humming and went back to stirring his curry. He supposed it would be nice to date someone better off than him, if he was going to date. There would be no worry if he lost his job, and he could live in Peter's fantastic place. Would that be so bad? Mikhail and Terrence seemed to enjoy their situation. It would mean he'd have to stop fucking other guys, and that would be a little strange, but they could still have an occasional threesome or something like that. Discussing that sounded like one of those 'communication' skills he needed to develop.

They ate in relative silence, partially because the curry was really damn good and also because Terrence was keeping tabs on the basketball game. Carson had never eaten curry before, and decided he needed to ask the fennec fox if it took a lot of effort. Even after a couple of helpings it didn't even look like they'd dented the amount in the pot.

"How much did you make?" Carson asked as he put his dishes into the dishwasher. It was one of the quiet models his mom had recently bought.

"I'll eat it for lunches for the rest of the next week," Mikhail said.

It never occurred to Carson to plan cooking. What else had he missed, having never lived with a boyfriend? Were there other skills that had waned? He knew how to decorate, in the sense of buying furniture that looked good, and things like laundry, but it seemed there was more to it. He'd always figured two gay guys living together was sort of like single life, except you fucked each other. Was there more to it?

"Can you pop that bottle for me?" the fennec asked. "Corkscrew is in the far left drawer."

The red fox was able to find it, and after some wiggling, got the bottle open with minimum bubbling over. For some reason, Mikhail had champagne flutes in one of the cabinets, so Carson poured out four glasses. Even if this was crazy alcoholic, and he suspected it would be, they had a driver. That was a weird thought to have.

"Cheers," Mikhail said, and all four of them clinked their glasses together. The tiny champagne flute looked miniature in Peter's paw, which made Carson smile.

"This is great," Terrence said after a few sips. He didn't seem sure how to properly drink it, since he kept looking over at everyone else. "Where'd you get it?"

"Ardennes, on 4th street," Peter answered.

"That's that ritzy place the boss gets all the fancy wine for our shows," the fennec said. He clinked his glass against the lion's own again. "I'll grab us something yummy next time I have to go by there."

Terrence looked like steam was about to come out of his ears from embarrassment, so Carson pretended not to notice. He pulled Peter around the corner, leaning up to kiss him on the cheek. It was so sudden he didn't even know why he did it. Was it the champagne? Was it the atmosphere? The only time he normally kissed someone was to break the tension as pants came down, or other people kissed him when they tied. This was something entirely new.

Carson and Peter said their goodbyes a few minutes later, after one more glass of champagne and Terrence mumbling out an invitation to come back two weeks from now for the next Strikers game. The fox knew the lion was extremely uncomfortable at the idea; why had they been invited back? Was it out of some sort of allegiance to him being a coworker? Was it because he remembered Mikhail from college? Hell, Carson felt he hid his discomfort at certain points very well, but Terrence just couldn't manage it. He decided to try another tactic once they were in Peter's limo.

"Why do you think he invited us back?" the fox asked. The bear was pressed up against him, even if there was more than enough room. One of Peter's big paws rested on his thigh.

"He wants to make friends too," the bear said. That paw slid to his inner thigh. Carson shivered. Marshall was a few feet away, patiently driving, with the partition down. With his other paw, the bear pressed a button, and the solid partition went up. It still felt very public to do anything here.

"It's only fifteen minutes to my apartment," Carson said, jumping up a little when the bear gripped his sheath through his pants.

"Then I will be quick," he said, and the fox felt his pants being undone. His cock was already getting hard, and one of the bear's paws reached into his underwear and pulled everything out into the air. He felt exposed, and was blushing hard, even if the idea was hot as hell. He'd always been the one to undo a driver's pants, grope him, or blow him as they sped to an apartment. There was one time it had been a race—if the wolf lasted to his garage, the fox would let him fuck him. They were driving down the road, and it was the fox's cock out this time. The bear started stroking him, and his knot expanded. It already felt like they wouldn't need all those minutes.

"Just relax," Peter whispered before he leaned over, nibbling on the fox's neck. Carson wrapped both his arms around the bear's shoulders. He didn't seem to want anything else right now—he just wanted to play with the fox in front of him, make him feel good. Was this payment for going with him to the movies? Would he get pounded later tonight by the bear?

He started humping up into the paw as he realized this wasn't 'for' anything. Peter just wanted him to feel good. The bear wouldn't even come up to his apartment—this was the end of the night, and it was there for the fox to enjoy. His knot was already full, and he was going to blow all over himself. Was this what being in a relationship was? Giving yourself to someone else, attending to them, and not expecting anything in return?

He whined to give some form of warning, and the bear took it, leaning down and taking the head of his cock between his lips right before he started to cum. Carson saw stars as the bear sucked hard, one paw still stroking his length. He shuddered, wiggling around despite his position, trying to not make any more noise in case it alerted Marshall to anything. It was like fucking back in college and trying not to wake up his roommate, and just as hot.

Peter pulled off, tucking the fox back in his clothes and re-buttoning his pants before Carson had even stopped breathing hard. A few drops of cum probably were going to stain the front of his underwear, but he was more impressed by what had just happened. Neither of the bear's paws were pushing him down into his lap, and though he could smell that the bear was aroused, he didn't seem to want anything. Hell, when the fox looked over, he could see the outline of the bear's cock in his pants, but he hadn't even unbuttoned.

The limo came to a stop, and the bear leaned over to kiss him on the lips. There wasn't tongue, or more groping—just a nice, sweet kiss after being jerked off. It was a strange mix of things, but he didn't have time to dwell now as the passenger-side door opened.

"Have a good night," Peter said as he broke the kiss.

Carson stumbled somewhat as he got out of the limo, and practically sprinted inside. He smelled entirely of sex, but that didn't bother him as much right now as what had just happened did. It wasn't the fooling around, or the kissing.

That had been a date, hadn't it? They'd gone to the movies, they'd visited a friend and enjoyed a few drinks, and then had some fun in the back of a car. It certainly hadn't been bad, but the fox wasn't sure what to do now. Did he call the bear? Did he text him? Whose move was it next? What happened now? He needed to calm down, and not think about this right now. Everything was so complicated. He'd just cum, so he needed something else to focus on.

It was amazing what was open at night in Papillon. In his old college town, a lot of stores closed at unreasonable hours, or weren't open at all when they thought their customers should be in church. Here, he could buy a cock ring at two in the morning if he wanted to. Right now, he wanted something filled with grease, salt, and self-loathing.

Stupid Peter and his stupid being charming. The fox walked into *Red 'n' White*, which was nearly deserted at this time of night. In another hour or two, the post-bar crowds would keep everyone busy, but in this golden hour, he could walk right up to the counter.

"Can I get..." he knew what he wanted, but he glanced at the pictures of the new burgers all the same. "...two Bacon Busters, a large fry, and a chocolate milkshake?" The wolf behind the counter inputted it into the register.

"That'll be $11.53," he said. The fox passed over a few bills and dropped his change in the tip jar.

It only took a few minutes to get his food, and then he rode back home. He didn't like eating this kind of stuff in front of others, especially since it took a while to get the grease out of the fur along his muzzle. Someone like a fennec fox could probably just use the little napkins in the restaurant, but he had to wash his face afterward.

His phone vibrated while he was riding back home, and a few more times while he took the elevator up to his floor. He didn't even look

Andres Cyanni Halden

at it until he was in his apartment, but his nose picked up something. There was a familiar scent in the air.

"Mom?" he called out. She was in the kitchen, a kettle in one paw.

"Oh, you got burgers," she said, walking back around the corner. "I'm making coffee."

"You should have told me you were coming over," he said, unpacking his bag on the table. She flicked her tail when she smelled the Bacon Busters. Carson's mom might be a health nut, but it was difficult for anyone to resist the smell of a burger containing deep-fried bacon strips.

"I sent you a text message an hour ago," his mom said. She set paper plates on the table, shaking out the fries on a paper towel. He checked his phone. Sure enough, she'd warned him about the same time as he'd been cumming in Peter's muzzle. While he had his phone open, he closed Knotz and quickly erased all his messages in case his mom looked over.

"I can't believe we still eat these," his mom muttered before unwrapping one of the burgers. She gave out a heavy sigh before taking a huge bite out of it.

"They're good," Carson said before unwrapping and starting to eat his own burger. The fries had spread out in a salty, greasy pile between their two plates.

"So what happened?" his mom asked. Carson coughed around a pickle slice. "I only buy these things when a guy doesn't call back. You always buy them when someone yells at you."

"It's a guy thing," he said after another bite.

"Is this that same bear?" his mom asked between French fries.

"Yeah," he replied. He took a few more bites.

"Did he do something freaky?" She was rapidly making sure he wasn't going to get any fries.

"No. He's nice…" That didn't even sound like a problem in the fox's head, so he tried to elaborate. "…and I don't know how to be nice back."

"What did he do? Show up at work?" she asked.

"No. We went out on a date…"

"That's good!" There went the last French fry.

"…and I don't know what to do now."

71

Carson finished his burger while he waited for his mom to answer. She knew much more about dating than he did. His mom had hooked up occasionally, but she'd also been married, and tended to prefer dating someone for a while over just ripping their pants off.

"I think you'll be fine," she said, picking up the plates and wrappers as she stood up. Even if she'd never lived here, she still felt the urge to clean up. "If you're scared, it means you know this is something different. Just don't do something stupid."

"Like what?" he asked. A variety of things sounded stupid right now.

"Well, if you're not exclusive right now, it's fine, but once you are, don't cheat on him. People think guys don't care as much, but they do. If he's nice, tell him what he did was nice. Don't be a dick just because you don't know what to do."

"Alright," he said, waiting for his mom to continue. She finished clearing the table before reaching into the bag and pulling out some moist towelettes.

"Here," she said, and threw him one. It would work for now, so he started trying to get the grease off his face. "He's foreign, right?"

"Russian," the fox explained.

"Enjoy that accent as long as you can," she commented as she poured them both a cup of coffee. "Aren't many foreign guys here, especially straight ones. I got a Latino fox last year and it was like winning the lottery."

# Chapter Six: ExecHowl and Dickensian

This guy's knot needed to shrink if he was going to get back to work on time.

The investment banker from a few streets down had his lunch hour free, so they decided to have some fun. Neither of them had really undressed—Carson had just pulled down his slacks enough to expose his ass, the wolf had just unbuckled his pants, and they went at it, draped across the back seat of the wolf's very nice car. It had tinted windows, and they were in a parking garage, so the odds of being caught were virtually nonexistent. However, now he regretted the decision, since one leg was cramping and he'd have to go back to work all stretched out. Normally he didn't mind it, but the knot was a bit much.

"Why did you tie?" Carson asked.

"Was just…" He grunted and tugged. "…in the moment," the wolf said. "You don't normally mind."

"I don't normally have to be at work in ten minutes," the fox said. His paw had been clenched around his phone, and he checked the time again. He had a few more messages, so he read text messages while the wolf took deep breaths and tried to calm himself down.

"Picking your next guy?" he said, and the fox folded his ears back. He hastily deleted all of the Knotz notifications and turned the app off.

"I was about to ask for a longer lunch break…" he groaned as the wolf popped out his half-deflated knot, the other canid letting out a low whine. "…but I guess we're good."

Carson clenched hard and rolled over to pull up his pants. The wolf tucked himself into his trousers and climbed up into the driver's seat.

"Drop you off at the bookstore?" the wolf asked as he turned the car back on.

"Sure," the fox said. He still had a few minutes. He could clean up in the bathroom, use some cologne, and normality would be achieved.

Luckily, there was no traffic, which gave the fox a little more time to straighten his clothes and look as presentable as possible. His phone buzzed while he was in the café's bathroom, and since Knotz was off, he figured his mom was sending him more vegetable pictures. After he felt he could go back to work, he checked his phone.

*Delivery for you at the customer service desk* read Terrence's message. That was odd. If his mom wanted to send him something, she'd just call and come over, or if she was busy, she'd drop it off at his apartment.

What awaited the fox stopped him in his tracks.

There was a bouquet of maroon roses in a dark purple vase, all brilliantly blooming, with a small card tucked in between two of the stems. When he stepped closer, he wondered why soaps and air fresheners had been lying to him about how roses smelled all these years. This was an entirely different experience; the mix of their natural aroma, the water in the vase, and the scent of a very familiar bear clung to the leaves.

"Peter send them?" Terrence asked.

"Seems like it…" He didn't really need to check the small card, but he did anyway to confirm Peter had sent them. They were very pretty, but they made his mind buzz.

Peter cared about him, enough at least to send him flowers at work to brighten his day, and the fox had taken a knot since the last time he'd seen the bear. Why couldn't he have just enjoyed last night? Why did he need to call a hookup at lunch today?

Primarily, the fox knew, was because he loved cock. College had been all about exploration, and he'd figured out what he liked very quickly. Maybe he needed to talk to Peter, try to tell him he wasn't looking for a relationship. The problem was, he wasn't sure if he actually disliked anything they did. This whole thing was just so new. Most people probably went through this kind of thing in high school, but he knew nothing about how to start a relationship, or how to maintain it, or how to break it off.

It couldn't be that difficult. Could he text Peter? Another question entered his mind—were they really dating? They had definitely gone out on a date, which was sort of the same thing. They'd had sex a few times, and it had been damn amazing. What if he made Peter mad? The fox couldn't really visualize the bear yelling, but the idea also made him uncomfortable. No matter how good he'd been at sucking cock, no one had ever sent him flowers. This was definitely something more.

74

He shifted the flowers so they didn't block access to the customer service desk, and even though looking at them made him feel a little bad about his sore tailhole, they did smell really good and almost every customer who talked to him commented on how pretty they were. And they were. He couldn't argue with that. He just felt they meant more.

It took him two hours to figure out what to text Peter. Something mad might have been the wrong decision, and he didn't want the bait and switch of sounding happy.

He settled on *I got your flowers.* It served its purpose.

*It was either that or a cock ring. I figured you would like the first one at work.* Came the response.

Carson sagged a little in relief. It was just a present. That was fine. It didn't mean anything.

*I think I owe you more than flowers.* Came the next text, which was quickly followed by a hastily-snapped pic of the bear's sheath. He could see a bathroom stall wall in the background.

"Can you help me?" someone asked. Carson immediately turned back around, all smiles. He could do this job right now, and deal with Peter later. The speaker was a remarkably fit older wolf.

"Absolutely. How can I assist you?"

The wolf looked to either side of him, and then folded back his ears. Even though he was easily in his fifties, the fox could see a blush forming on his throat.

"I need...a book."

"Who is the author?" Carson politely asked. He had a pretty good idea what this was about. Only a few people acted this shy in a bookstore.

"...Sergio Kingdom," the customer whispered.

"Let me look that up for you..." the fox typed the name in, and swiveled the screen to face the wolf.

"That one," he said, pointing at the screen. Carson swiveled it back around, exited the window, and then smiled at the wolf.

"Give me just a minute, sir, and I'll find that book for you."

Being in Papillon meant they catered to the area, and besides the large children's section, that meant an extensive collection of gay books. The vast majority of these were the 'How to Come Out to your Family/Friends/Coworkers/Wife-Before-You-Divorce' varieties, but a good chunk also catered to more personal tastes.

Dozens of BDSM anthologies lined the highest shelf in the 'Mature Viewing' section, with *Great Gay Erotica* Volumes 1-20 barely out of a child's reach. Books with titles like *Kitty Cat Craves Cock* and *Tied!* filled every shelf. There was the wolf's book, *Great Gay Sex for Canines over Forty*, sandwiched in between *The Rabbit Kama Sutra* and *Trim Those Claws: Gay Sex Secrets for Big Cats*. He walked back to his desk, setting the book cover-down on the counter.

"If you'd like, we can ship any other books discreetly to your home," Carson offered, watching the wolf's ears perk up at the word 'discreetly.'

"Can I do that...with this one?" he asked. Poor guy didn't even want to be seen walking out of the store with it. His boyfriend/husband must think everything was fine.

"We can ship anything you need, especially if we already have it in-store," the fox said. "If you live in St. Marx, you'll receive it within a day."

Now the wolf looked excited. "Can you go grab me all the others too, then? I mean, the other books by him."

"No problem."

A few minutes later, he carried the wolf's books to the line of cashiers, whispering into Richard's ear to not say any of the titles out loud. After the coyote blushed, Carson watched the two be all flustered at each other for a bit until the wolf had paid for his books and walked over to the café. Richard signaled to one of the other cashiers, a new tigress named Claudia, that he was taking his break. She did her job and didn't really socialize. That was fine by him.

"That was weird," Richard said, his tail wagging despite what was left of his blush while he walked over for a coffee. They got half off at the bistro here, so nearly everyone ordered something on their breaks.

"We sell a lot of porn books," the fox said, figuring since Terrence was on lunch and no one was currently at the customer service desk he could grab a quick cup. His stomach growled, reminding him lunch hadn't exactly happened either. He'd grab a muffin as well.

"I didn't really...expect that," the coyote said. Well, he was getting better. A week ago, he would have just blushed and refused to talk about anything. Maybe Papillon made him comfortable now instead of nervous.

"It's why we all have jobs," Carson continued. "We sell more gay sex books than bestsellers."

"Is it just because of where we are?" he asked.

"Yup. Large Latte." The first word he said to Richard, the second sentence to Mark. The foxhound gave him his best 'I'd love to fuck you' smile, but it didn't work on Carson.

"Can you bring this over to my desk?" he asked. The coyote nodded, so the fox rushed back to work as a deer mom tugged a toddler toward his station. Parents did not have spare patience for him.

After ordering the book for her, the fox sipped his coffee. Weirdly, Richard was shopping during his off-time. The only reason Carson still bought books here was because of his employee discount, and then he'd do it while he was on shift. It was easy enough to look up a book at his desk and then retrieve while doing something else for a customer. Of course, since getting this job, he read a lot less. In the same sense, he suspected people that worked in chocolate factories ate vegetables at home.

"The Shelf Life down on 4th Avenue closed," Richard commented. Carson had worked there before. They didn't have a café, and were sandwiched between two movie theaters. It didn't surprise him.

"How much longer do you think we have?" the coyote asked. The fox took a sip from his latte before answering.

"We'll be fine," he said. "The people with kids bring them in for the readings, and the adults buy porn." He knew his mom bought her porn digital, but he didn't need to hide his. Then again, her last roommate had been a prude, while he preferred to live alone. Shelf Life had also been five times the size of this place, and employed damn near a hundred people. There were less than a dozen employees here. Terrence kept it that way, so profits were high and he could profit-share with everyone. It also worked well for Carson, since he needed to remember fewer names.

"I heard Patrick Pratt is gonna do a signing here," Richard said.

"Tomorrow," the fox said. "He'll be here for a few hours. We're all on the schedule."

"Why's that?"

"Security," the fox said after another sip. "He tends to get mobbed by middle-aged ladies."

"Cause he's an author?"

Setting his latte down, Carson walked over to the new releases section. He picked up a copy of *Bone to Pick*, and opened the back cover. It showed a picture of a middle-aged, quite attractive black fox dressed in a business suit, grinning and staring with his dusty-gray eyes.

"He's cute," Richard mumbled, blushing profusely.

"He also has an English accent."

"...wow." He could guess what the coyote was thinking about, since Carson shared some of those fantasies. The fox had this idea that Pratt might be gay, since he was still single and never hooked up with any of the women that threw themselves at him. Maybe he'd get a chance to ask.

"He flew all the way over here?" Richard asked while they walked back to the customer service desk.

"He lives in St. Marx," Carson said. "He always does a few bookstores in town when his book tours start."

"Oh, ok," the coyote said before heading back to his register. The fox noticed his coworker had left a small piece of paper on the customer service desk. Curiosity getting the better of him, he unfolded it. It said 'Dick223'. Smirking, the fox typed it into Knotz. The profile was definitely a coyote. He didn't want to fuck Richard, but the least he could do was politely turn him down.

Once the fox got home, he set the vase of flowers on his kitchen counter and just stared at them. This was a problem. He didn't want to be monogamous. He liked Peter fine, and he definitely liked Peter's cock, but the bear needed to know that was the end of it. Then again, he knew Peter was definitely fucking other people. Did he just like the fox best, or was this just how he operated? Maybe the guys in the pictures on his phone got flowers as well, but for some reason the fox doubted it. Peter liked him, probably more than the fox expected.

Did that bother him? A few weeks ago, it might have, or if Peter was bad in bed it definitely would. However, here was a nice guy who had a big cock. What was wrong with that? Couldn't he just see where things would go? He definitely felt something for the bear, even if he didn't really know how to describe it. He could worry about it some other time. The flowers were pretty, and he needed to get some sleep before work tomorrow.

The next morning started out fine, even though Carson knew the workday would be ridiculous. A submissive tiger had blown him a few minutes before he rode off to work, so even if he got trampled by menopausal moms, at least he'd die satisfied. Richard and Claudia paced back and forth outside the doors, making sure the housewives and occasional gay guy formed an orderly line. Most of the fans clutched hardcovers to their chests, or chattered eagerly with the person closest to them. Rather than have to answer questions, the fox pedaled behind the store, locked his bike to the box compactor, and walked in, making sure he picked up his larger-font nametag from Terrence's desk as he walked by.

The lion chatted in a hushed tone with Patrick Pratt near the closed front doors, and he could see a few housewives through the windows, trying to figure out what they were discussing. When Carson walked by, intent on buying a cup of coffee before everything officially opened, he caught a snippet of the conversation.

"...and we'll keep everything moving smoothly," the lion said.

"That's just fine, Mr. Lawson. Just remind your customers that a personalization needs to be short and sweet," Pratt said. Christ, Carson could listen to him recite a grocery list. He wasn't just British, he had those wonderful tones that made everything he said sound smooth and soothing. He was even leaning on a silver-tipped cane. The author flicked an ear when Carson walked past.

"Would you mind grabbing me a black coffee?" he asked, passing the red fox a five-dollar-bill.

"Sure," he said, but before he could take another step, Terrence held up his paws.

"Everything's gratis, Mr. Pratt," he said quickly, but the black fox shook his muzzle.

"I insist," Pratt said. Carson escaped before he would be pulled into the conversation further.

A minute later he had two cups of black coffee in his paws, and set one down on Pratt's long table. The author was setting a line of pens out in front of him, one black and the rest forming a rainbow.

79

"I suspect a few residents of Papillon will appreciate this," Pratt said. He smiled, and Carson found himself blushing. The author had to know how charismatic he was. Otherwise, this level of easy charm would be unfair.

"My mom really likes your books," the fox blurted out, feeling embarrassed. He didn't get flustered when a bull fucked him in a gym shower, but a smiling fox in a suit could flabbergast him.

"A lot of people's mums do," Pratt said with a smile. "Want me to sign the new one for her?"

"She's probably in line," he mumbled, leaning over to look out the window. Since she hadn't called him last night to ask him to skip the line, she was probably here with her friends.

"Well, how about this," he said, picking up the top book from his personal stack of *Bone to Pick*. "You got me coffee. I can give you something."

"You paid for it," Carson said, but the smile didn't disappear.

"You still got it for me." He flipped open the front of the hardcover. "What's your mum's favorite color?"

"Green," he said automatically, watching as the author picked up the emerald-colored pen, and after giving it a good shake, scribbled on the crisp page.

"Here," he said, blowing on the cover for a moment before closing the book and holding it out to Carson. He took it, and read the inscription.

*To a wonderful mother:*
*You are loved.*

*Patrick Pratt*

"Thanks," he whispered. His mom might die of happiness.

"I won't be as charming when I meet her, I promise," Pratt said. "I won't know which mum she is, after all."

"I'll be at the customer service desk if you need anything from the back of the store," Carson said, and the other fox nodded as Terrence unlocked the front door.

Most customers stayed quiet, and since every employee was here, there were enough witnesses to curb shoplifting and keep everything moving. When someone tried to ask Patrick Pratt a multitude of questions, Richard or Claudia politely moved them along. Most of Carson's job right now was to keep books flowing—Terrence had moved Pratt's entire backlog to the fox's desk. He passed paperback after paperback to customers eager to get in line, reminding them they needed to pay for their books before stepping outside to the line. A few thieves had probably gotten through, since so many housewives had brought their own books, but with them selling hundreds of more books than usual, it wasn't as big of a loss.

Carson was only able to leave his desk once the entire morning, and that was to retrieve another box of paperbacks from the back room. Their next quarterly bonus would be huge at this rate. While he was unpacking it—the books he set on the counter disappearing into customers' paws almost as quickly—he watched as the signing line slowed to a halt. Terrence cupped both paws around his muzzle.

"Patrick Pratt will be taking a short break," he called out. "Please feel free to walk around the store and visit our café." Carson watched as the black fox shook one more paw before standing up and walking over to the café. The red fox's phone buzzed as he helped a customer pick a paperback for Pratt to sign.

*Well look at that,* said a message from Knotz. The fox opened the profile attached to it and felt a blush creep up his throat. The pictures showed a black fox from behind, bracing a familiar cane across his ass.

*I guess that answers why you don't fuck housewives,* Carson sent back. He helped a few more customers before a response buzzed.

*I don't sleep with married people,* Pratt sent, *and since you are on here, I assume you are not attached.* He realized the voice in his head while he read the message even had that smooth accent. Well, he'd send Peter pictures if he could. The black fox might not post pictures of his cock for the public, but he wondered if the millionaire author would mind if he took home some souvenirs.

*I leave here an hour after you do.* He sent.

*I have a townhouse in the Historic District* the other fox sent back. Carson could easily bike there. He helped a few more customers as he watched Pratt sit back down at the signing table. He was slick; the red fox could see him tapping at his cell phone screen without looking at it.

*Be there whenever you'd like. You could spend the night, if you'd prefer.* Pratt sent. That was an idea. He still hadn't slept at Peter's place, but then again, he couldn't be tied to the bear either. When was the last time he'd fallen asleep with a knot in him? For some reason, he couldn't visualize the author as a bottom. Maybe it was the cane.

*Sounds good.* He wondered what the black fox used as dirty talk.

"Patrick Pratt will begin signing again!" Terrence bellowed out into the store. "Those that left the line, please return with your vouchers to avoid moving to the back of the line!"

There was still an orderly group of housewives winding out and around the store, so Carson focused on doing his job. They were most likely going to sell out of every Pratt book in the store, which meant bigger bonuses for everyone. The red fox even noticed a lot of people buying whatever Richard or Claudia recommended, so their whole thriller section would need to be re-stocked this week. Maybe that cute husky would stop by. He could always go for an eager dog in the back of the delivery van. Carson came out of his fantasy when Richard set a cup of coffee on his counter.

"I need your help outside. Terrence ordered more Pratts from a local bookstore, and they're heavy," the coyote said.

"Sure thing," the fox said. "Get Claudia to cover my desk."

He might have suspected Claudia was stronger than him, since she was damn near six feet tall and pretty muscular, but she was also the newest employee. She didn't deal with the other bookstores in the area.

"Hey, Otome," Carson said as he walked up to the pickup parked on the street. A red panda in a purple suit started to undo bungee cords that held down a dozen boxes in the bed of the truck.

"This is mostly *Bone to Pick,*" Otome said. "Some paperbacks."

"No problem. Are these from the 4th or 7th Street store?" Carson asked. Otome was the owner of Nakamura Books, which had a few dozen locations in the state.

"Both," he said, and pulled out a thick sheaf of papers. "Give these to Terrence. He's lucky Pratt isn't coming to any of my stores this year." Carson suspected Otome had charged Terrence more than he should have, but he didn't say anything as he took the invoices in one paw and a box of books under the other arm.

"You want to talk to him?" Carson asked. Otome peeked through one of the windows, and then shook his muzzle.

"He looks busy. Just make sure he pays me."

Finances might not be part of the fox's workload, but he knew better than to argue about hundreds of dollars' worth of books. It took a few minutes to get everything moved into the store, the hardcovers going straight to Pratt's table and the paperbacks scattered at the customer service desk. Fans were still rabid, which meant they disappeared almost as fast as they were being unpacked. With this bonus check, Carson might be able to treat Peter to dinner. That was an odd idea to have, he thought, but the look on the rich bear's face from someone else paying would be worth it.

The store had authors here most weeks, and with the exception of the children's authors, Pratt was the most patient he'd ever seen. He didn't even frown when someone walked around the table for a picture. Carson had seen a Texan romance author here a few months ago who nearly punched a customer over that. However, Pratt just smiled, signed books, and hugged customers. It definitely helped sales.

Patrick Pratt finally stood up, waving to the amassed group. A few people who'd failed to receive signatures groaned, but nearly everyone else clapped. A text message buzzed in his pocket, so while the black fox packed up, the fox turned away to read.

*Why didn't you tell me Pratt was going to be here?* Read a text from his mom. The fox's tail flared. He looked around, trying to figure out where she was. He loved his mom very much, but he sure as Hell didn't want her at his job.

*I got you a book.* He sent back. Maybe she would leave.

Nope, there she was. Carson's mom was in the coffee shop, wearing a neon orange, tie-dyed sundress, and looking ready to throw Patrick Pratt down on one of the little bistro tables and do unspeakable things to him. To the author's credit, he kept smiling, and wasn't brandishing his cane at her. Carson ran toward them.

"...and I just loved in *Exposed Bone* how Detective Madison figured out the connection between Sanders and Miguel..." Carson suspected there was going to be a lot more to this conversation if he didn't break it up. He placed a paw on his mom's shoulder, which got her to turn around. He pressed the hardcover book into her paws before she could say anything.

"You got the first signature," he told her, looking over her shoulder at Pratt. He was smirking.

"Your mother was telling me all about her favorite books," the author said, taking a sip of a new cup of coffee. "She's quite the firecracker."

"Thanks?" Carson said. No one he'd ever fucked had met his mother, at least not intentionally. There was Mr. Gonzales, but that didn't really count, since that had been years before they'd hooked up, not hours.

"You wouldn't believe what he's been telling me about the next few books!" his mom squeaked out. Carson was afraid she was going to explode any second, so he steered her away, flipping the book open in her paws.

"Enjoy, mom. Mr. Pratt's been signing for hours. He needs a break from fans." Maybe that would work, especially as his mom read the dedication. She stopped moving, and gave a little sniffle.

"That's so sweet," she whispered, and gave Carson a hug, much to his embarrassment. Someone would see him, he knew it. Maybe they'd think he was dating an older woman. That'd be fine, as long as they didn't think his mommy visited him at work.

"I need you and Claudia to put up the signing table and move the shelves back into place," Terrence said behind him. "Hi, Vicky."

"Hi, Terrence!" she said, detaching to hug the fox's boss. Now he had no idea what was going on, and ducked away to do as ordered.

"How's your mother doing?" she asked, and now it started to click together. She had friends all over the city, from various Tupperware parties and book clubs. Well, he sincerely hoped they were Tupperware parties and not passion parties. He knew his mom had sex. He knew his mom owned sex toys. That didn't mean he wanted to think about it.

Claudia was indeed a lot stronger than him. The only reason he ended up being there was for balance, since muscles in her arms bulged as she shifted the bookcases across the hardwood floor with ease. She also took direction well, which Carson liked in a new employee. Maybe he could get her to load the book carts tomorrow.

His shift ended a few minutes later, and the fox wondered what he should do prior to visiting Pratt. Shower, certainly, but food sounded like a good idea, and he didn't really want to eat alone, or with his mother. Once he locked up his bike, Carson pulled out his phone.

*Want to grab some Chinese food?* He sent to Richard while he rode the elevator up.

*Sure.* He sent back almost immediately. *I'll be at your apartment in…20 mins?*

During the intervening time, the red fox took a shower, and then wiggled into a tight t-shirt and ass-hugging jeans. If he was going to hook up with a famous author, he was going to look damn sexy and make the black fox drool, if that was in an English fox's nature. He was at least going to try to make him break his cool, since he'd done little more than charmingly smirk even while inviting the red fox over for a little cock. Then, he texted the coyote to ask what he wanted to eat. A minute later, Richard arrived wearing a turtleneck, despite the fact is was barely sixty degrees outside.

"Where are you from?" the fox asked.

"Panama," he said. "I didn't think it would be so damn cold up here."

"We're not in Canada," Carson said. "My dad lives in Vancouver. It's awful."

"Snow?" the coyote said, his ears back.

"All the fucking time," the fox said.

Richard shuddered. "Some of the people at work today were crazy," the coyote said, changing the subject. Carson pulled out a few bitch beers from the fridge, popping them with the edge of the counter. They clinked them together and flopped down on the couch while they waited for the Chinese delivery guy to get here.

"Did you have to deal with Cat Sweater Lady?" Carson asked.

Richard's eyes went wide. "I thought I was the only one!"

"She's at every big signing. She's always touching stuff, fucking up shelves, demanding weird stuff from the café…" Carson said.

"Why doesn't Terrence kick her out?" Richard asked.

"She spends *so* much money," Carson explained. "Today she bought three hundred dollars' worth of hardcovers and four coffees."

"Christ," he said, taking a swig. The intercom buzzed, so the fox got up to answer it. He'd be nice today and pay for dinner. Besides, the coyote had ordered one of the cheapest things on the menu.

They ate in silence for a few minutes, except for each of them giggling at the other struggling with chopsticks. He had to go get them forks.

"So..." the coyote said to his lo mein.

"So what?" the fox asked. The fox was draped over half the couch, while the coyote leaned against the opposite armrest. Also, the coyote's blush was obvious even from this distance.

"Did you...look at my page?" Richard asked, and the fox set down his fork.

"I didn't invite you over to fuck you," the fox said simply, and frowned when the coyote physically relaxed.

"Is that why you thought..." Dammit, the fox thought. He knew he had a lot of sex, but every interaction didn't need to include a cock in his mouth. Then again, up until a few weeks ago, it basically had. Richard had given him his page info, which meant the coyote wanted to fool around with him. He wanted to, sure, but he also didn't want the kid to rush into it. Fuck, he wasn't the kid's parent. If he wanted to whip his dick out, that was his business. Besides, he was cute. What would it hurt?

Carson realized why it bothered him. An anonymous hookup was one thing; there weren't any emotions involved. However, it was really obvious the coyote had a crush on him. He'd be breaking the kid's heart if he fucked him and then didn't want anything else. He didn't want to date the coyote, and he wasn't even sure he wanted to fuck him on a regular basis. Even if he wasn't, the fox had the impression Richard was a virgin, or at least inexperienced. It was hot to think about teaching him things, but he didn't want to hurt his feelings.

"We're not going to fuck," the fox finally said. Now the coyote looked crestfallen, so he quickly added, "you are cute, but I've already got a boyfriend."

"You're still on Knotz," the coyote said, and the fox nodded.

"Yeah, but have you even hooked up with anyone on it? Or are you just looking at the cock pictures?" Carson asked. Judging by how fast the coyote's blush came back, he could guess.

"That's what I thought," the fox said, standing up, picking up their paper plates and walking to the kitchen. "Look, I know you're not used to having a lot of gay guys around you, but that's most of the area. If you want a boyfriend, go find a boyfriend." Who was he to give this kind of advice? Honestly, he didn't think he had any credentials, but he knew he liked being around Peter. There was a difference between just fucking someone and spending time to get to know them. The coyote obviously wanted the latter.

"I..." the coyote said, and then looked back down. Carson walked around the couch and gave him a hug.

"How about we hit *Honeypot* tomorrow night? It's down on 14th. Lots of cute guys there." The fox offered. "I'll invite Peter. You can meet someone."

"Ok," the coyote said, hugging him back before the fox detached.

"And remember to log out of Knotz when other people can see your phone. There's a wolf cock on your screen."

The ride to the Historic District gave the red fox time to think, since there wasn't much traffic. Maybe it would be best if he stopped using Knotz. He had guaranteed sex with Peter, and it was nice to just be around the bear. It shouldn't be that difficult to find someone to fuck outside of the app, especially if he was going to start clubbing. Richard would find someone to date, and the fox could find someone to bring back to Peter's apartment for them to have a freaky threesome. Well, he supposed a threesome wasn't too freaky, but it would definitely be hot to watch the bear fuck someone in front of him.

He knocked on the townhouse door, hearing footfalls on the other side. Pratt met him at the door, dressed in a dark blue silk robe tied loosely at the waist. Carson smiled.

Pratt leaned on a different cane, and reminded the fox of a few porn movies he'd seen over the years. Of course, the intricately-carved, ivory pipe sticking out of one side of his muzzle definitely helped the impression that the red fox was going to enjoy this. Pratt took the pipe out from between his lips.

"I can put it out if you'd like," the black fox said. Carson actually liked the smell of tobacco, and it also reminded the red fox of his first trip in Peter's car. He didn't need to think about the bear right now. There was an attractive black fox standing right in front of him, ready and willing.

"I like it," he said with a smirk, shutting the door behind him. He threw off his windbreaker, and the black fox padded back toward a large armchair situated in the middle of the room.

When the fox looked around, he wondered if every author lived like this. Books lined every wall from floor to ceiling, and the scent of old paper even overtook the scent of the pipe once he walked further into the townhouse. Around a corner, he could only see more bookshelves and even small books in frames on the staircase to his right. There must be thousands of them, some old, some newer, but all together creating an atmosphere of comfort. The black fox had sprawled out in the large armchair, his robe undone, showing off completely black fur, with the tip of his cock already escaping his sheath. He was a little chubby, but Carson didn't mind. The other fox took a few puffs from the pipe and blew rings into the air.

"Come here, then," Pratt said, but this time Carson heard the edge of control in it. The red fox figured he'd be on bottom in this situation, and the black fox practically confirmed it, so without taking off his pants he just knelt in front of the chair.

The black fox responded fast to Carson licking across his sheath. It didn't take him long to get completely hard, and when his knot started to form, Pratt put a paw on the back of Carson's head. He took the hint, sliding his lips over the head and working his way down. He wasn't that big, but the fox preferred that to being too big to fit comfortably in his muzzle. The red fox started to bob, one paw wrapping around the other fox's knot. When he looked up, he watched the black fox take a puff from his pipe, smiling down at him.

"Oh, you brought someone home," said a voice. Carson went to pull off, but the paw on the back of his head held him in the black fox's lap. When he looked up again, a gray-furred rabbit was in his field of vision, giving the black fox a kiss on the cheek. Then, the rabbit walked around behind him.

"Do keep going," Pratt said, in his most charming voice. Carson moaned around the cock in his mouth when a paw gripped his sheath through his pants. He wasn't much for threesomes, and he especially didn't want it to be a surprise. Those roaming paws undid his jeans and shoved them down, and he smelled lube when he heard a bottle pop open. Shit, this wasn't what he'd expected at all.

What felt weirdest about right now is that he couldn't really complain. He'd come over here for cock, and here was cock, in his muzzle and about to be in his ass. In signing up for Knotz, and following a relative stranger home, he knew stuff like this could happen. A surprise threesome wasn't even the worst thing that could have occurred.

Fingers pressed against his tailhole, and it did feel good, he had to admit, even if he didn't know anything about the rabbit. He'd looked at the pictures on Pratt's profile. He knew for a fact the black fox had a lot of things off-limits, and had a note reading 'No Names Please'. Carson didn't mind anonymity, but he wanted to know something about someone who fucked him. He tried to keep consistently bobbing his head, but he had to pause and relax when the rabbit started to push into him, his lubed paw wrapping around the red fox's cock.

Fuck, this rabbit had no rhythm. He wasn't big, but he just started pounding fast, his paw on Carson's cock not stroking in sync. It felt good, sure, but it could feel a lot better, especially when he was trying to blow Pratt. Since the rabbit obviously didn't know he was doing anything wrong, the fox wiggled his hips, trying to get a better angle. When he looked up at Pratt again, the black fox smiled, his other paw now tapping out the pipe. The black fox just leaned his head back, letting out a happy sigh. He was enjoying this show, even if Carson was very sure he wouldn't be coming back.

The only warning he got from Pratt was the paw on the back of his head gripping a little harder. The black fox's cock twitched, a second later shooting cum into his muzzle. Carson swallowed quickly, squeezing Pratt's knot with one paw. He let out a whine, and the red fox kept bobbing his head, listening to the black fox whimper. Lots of guys got really sensitive when they came, and especially right after, so he didn't stop until Pratt's hips started wiggling and he yelped.

Carson lifted his muzzle off Pratt's cock, breathing hard as the rabbit pounded hard, until he felt him slam in as deep as possible. The rabbit came, the paw on the fox's cock stroked fast, and a second paw gave his knot a hard squeeze, practically forcing him to cum along with him. He liked to cum at his own pace, and even if it felt physically good, he knew he wanted to leave as soon as he could.

The rabbit pulled out, which let Carson shakily stand up. His cock was slick with lube and cum, and he could clench pretty hard, especially since there wasn't a tie to worry about. He yanked his pants up, tucking himself back into them. No one said anything. Maybe that's what irritated him most about what had just happened. No one asked him if he had liked it. Neither of them even sarcastically apologized for springing a rabbit on him.

He slammed the front door behind him.

When he was outside in the cool air, it didn't help his mood. The fox didn't want to go home, and he definitely didn't want to go to a bar. Only one option came to mind.

He biked into downtown, realizing how difficult it was to ride a bike comfortably with a load of cum inside him. Generally he didn't notice due to the euphoria, but right now he was just really pissed. The breeze would pull off the scent, but he needed a shower badly. His phone buzzed, and he mentally yelled at it.

It was all that damn app's fault. Without it, he could have learned to date. He could have learned all the normal grown-up skills about how to date other people, what physical cues to pick up on, when to call someone back. Instead, he'd purchased a smartphone and let it substitute real life. All because he figured if he could have all the cock he wanted, why not?

He knew it wasn't Knotz's fault, or his phone's fault. It was his. He'd made the decision to suck random cocks instead of learning how to date, and hooking up with hot wolves in cars instead of going to dinner to talk about books. He couldn't blame anyone but himself, and maybe that was what made him the angriest about the whole situation.

There weren't bike racks in the Carter Building's parking garage, but there were support pillars, so he locked his bike to one of them. If he remembered correctly, Marshall had needed a key to take the elevator up to the bear's apartment. When he pressed the elevator button, it immediately opened for him.

This place might be a fancy apartment building, but it was still a place where people lived and got surprise visitors and deliveries.

When he looked at the panel with all the floor buttons, he noticed one at the bottom labeled 'Call'. On an educated guess, he pressed that one and the button for the sixty-seventh floor. It took about thirty seconds for an answer to come through.

"I cannot have any clients up right..." Peter started.

"It's me," the fox said into the tiny speaker. He realized his voice cracked a little.

"Oh," came the reply. "Press the button again. Elevator will come up."

The bear hadn't asked him why he was here, or what he wanted. He'd just buzzed him up. Was this what being in a relationship was? Carson wondered what might be happening that would stop him from seeing people, but right now he didn't care. He just wanted someone to be nice to him, and not just because he sucked cock.

When the elevator doors opened, the bear was there to meet him. He smelled strongly of scotch and cigars, which only somewhat covered up the underlying scent of sex. Carson could probably guarantee the bear had a better night than him. The fox just stepped out of the elevator and hugged him, burying his face in Peter's fur. He only wore a housecoat, and it wasn't tied closed. His fur smelled more like sex, but right now the fox didn't care.

"You alright?" Peter asked.

Carson figured there was no point in lying, "No," he said.

"You want a drink?" the bear whispered. Why was he whispering?

"Is someone else here?" the fox asked.

"Yes," the bear responded. "And he is asleep on couch."

"You have any scotch left?"

"Always," Peter said.

"Then yes."

While the bear went into the kitchen to pour the fox's drink, Carson stepped into the living room. On the coffee table sat two empty glasses that smelled strongly of scotch, and a few cigars sitting in an ash tray. Who was sprawled over the couch, however, was much more interesting.

There was Marshall, naked, his belly smeared with shots of cum, snoring lightly. One of his legs dangled over the edge, the toes almost touching the carpet. Overcome with curiosity, the fox took a step closer, and now he could smell Peter on him as well. The dog sniffed

91

in his sleep and rolled over, his tail wagging a few times, and now it was quite obvious Peter had topped him as well. The dog wiggled a little before he let out a sigh and started to breathe evenly again.

"Sorry you have to see this," Peter whispered behind him, making the fox jump.

"How often does this…" he waved at the dog. "…happen?" Peter shrugged.

"Every few months. We find out about a new whiskey, we share, I end up fucking him. He is not dating anyone, and we said we were open."

"I don't care about that," the fox said, but when he thought about it, he did. He wondered now what the bear thought about him sleeping around. "He's your butler."

"He is also my friend," the bear said, giving the fox the full glass of scotch. Peter did not skimp when it came to alcohol.

"I want it to be just us," the fox whispered, taking a long drag from the glass and walking back into the kitchen. He didn't want to talk about monogamy with a passed-out, fucked bull terrier in front of him.

"You are mad at me?" the bear asked, kissing him on the side of the neck.

"No," Carson said, and sighed, taking another swig. The scotch would help him sleep and not much else right now. He was so mad, so frustrated and just fed up with other people at the moment.

"So, you want us to be boyfriends?" Peter said, his lips tracing down to the fox's shoulder, even if he still had his shirt on.

"Yes," the fox said, shivering. Dammit, he'd just cum a few minutes ago and the bear was threatening to get him hard again. He wanted to make things clear, and then he wanted to go to sleep.

"Ok," Peter said, and took a few steps until he was in front of the fox. He leaned down, and kissed the fox on the lips. There wasn't any tongue, and there were no gropes. It was just a simple, loving kiss that meant a lot more than a paw down his pants.

"You taste like a fox," the bear said after he pulled back. Carson blushed under his fur. He figured the scotch would have covered that up.

"It wasn't a very good night," Carson commented. He leaned against the bear, closing his eyes.

"I smell rabbit too. You have better night than me. I only make one guy squeal."

Despite everything that had happened in the last few hours, Carson started to giggle. When he tried to be quiet, it didn't help at all, and he just let it all out. It had been a bad night, but Peter didn't even care. He just wanted him to feel better, and had tried to lighten the mood. That was enough, the fox thought.

They drained their glasses, and Peter led him into the bedroom. The beautiful, giant bed was still there, but the fox had other needs right now.

"Shower," he said, and the bear shut the bedroom door, and then walked into the bathroom. None of the lights were on, but it didn't matter with the huge windows. Carson started undressing, wondering what he would wear to work tomorrow. At the moment, the fox didn't care. When Peter turned on the water, the fox stretched to pop his back, then walked into the large bathroom.

Peter was already under the shower heads, his fur soaked down, smiling over at the fox through the many streams. Carson couldn't help but smile back. It was a very nice shower, and he didn't mind the company, especially now.

The bear's huge paws turned him toward the spouts, and while his fur got soaked, he felt one of the big paws sliding under his tail. A finger found his tailhole, and even if he wasn't too sore, he did wince a little in remembering the terrible rabbit. Peter would be gentle. He was always gentle.

"I want to take you," the bear rumbled. He wrapped his other arm around the fox's waist. "I want to show you I care about you."

Carson's body responded before his mind did. Even if it hadn't been very long at all, his sheath started to fill, and he pressed back against the naked bear. They could have a little time. They could do whatever they wanted tonight. He could worry about relationships and monogamy and how dating worked tomorrow. Right now, he wanted Peter to hold him, and take care of him, and for him not to have to care about anything. So, he nodded.

He never knew how Peter got hard so fast, but he felt the thick length pressing into him. He pressed back. The rabbit, however unpleasant, had stretched him out, so the fox was able to take the thick length without much of a problem. Peter gasped and kissed his ears, the back of his neck, practically anywhere he could reach when he bottomed out in the fox.

"Grip the showerheads," the bear whispered, and the fox reached up. The fixtures were secure in the tile, and he moaned loudly as the bear pulled back and thrust back in. He might as well be suspended in the air, since his toes barely touched the ground.

Each of the bear's thrusts made him arch his back and moan. He was hard, but he didn't care right now. Peter was showing how much he cared about him with every rock of his hips and every movement of his paws. They roamed all over him, sometimes giving his knot a squeeze, gripping his hips, his shoulders, sometimes pinching his nipples. It was more loving than the wolf day trader whom he'd known for years, and more erotic than the horse who was into spanking. This was making love, and he didn't need strawberries or satin sheets to do it.

Peter never stopped kissing him. At one point, he even turned the fox's muzzle so they could kiss on the lips. Carson felt shaky, but he knew the bear wouldn't let him fall. One paw gripped his waist, and the other kept stroking his cock. He was going to cum all over the shower wall, and he'd love every second of it.

He came, squeezing hard around the cock inside him. Peter bit down on the back of his neck, and the fox practically howled as he felt him and the bear cumming together. He gripped the showerheads, lifting himself up off the ground and putting as much pressure as he could on the bear's cock. He wanted to feel every inch, every twitch, and every drop of cum. The bear let go of his scruff, kissing it before growling deep in his throat.

"Down," he gasped out, and the fox would have slumped to the shower floor completely if there wasn't an arm around his waist. The bear pulled out, giving the fox's sensitive cock a few more strokes as he did so. Carson could barely stand up, but the smell of the rabbit and black fox were definitely gone. That had felt amazing, and the thought of being able to do it whenever he wanted was definitely a promising idea.

Peter turned on the dryers, and since the fox was a little dazed, the bear turned him around, kissing across his muzzle while his fur dried out. He'd love to stand like this until morning, but the post-coital exhaustion was kicking in. He closed his eyes while he pressed against the bear, glad for someone to hold who didn't think he was slutty enough to spring a threesome on.

When he opened his eyes, he realized the bear must have carried him to bed. Peter climbed in next to him, pulling the sheets over them.

"Thanks," Carson whispered. The bear kissed him on one ear.

"Spokoinai Nochi," Peter whispered back. Whatever that meant, the fox was happy.

# Chapter Seven: \<Are You Sure?\>

Carson was sore when he woke up. His ass hurt, his arms felt tingly, and when he rolled over, he winced as the quick drying last night yanked out a few hairs. Peter was still asleep beside him, and he could smell frying bacon. Why could he smell bacon? He sat up, popped his shoulder, and went to roll out of bed when an arm wrapped around him.

"Five minutes," the bear said, and was pulled back against him. He felt Peter's erection press against his rear, but there was no way that was going to happen this morning. The bear kissed his ears.

"You are sure about it being just us?" he whispered.

The events of last night came back to him in a bit more detail. He knew he'd said that in a fit of anger and frustration, but he'd meant it. He'd just hooked up with a famous author, gone to his house, and essentially whored himself out. Before going to Pratt's house, he'd never considered himself slutty, and now he wanted to see what being with just one person would be like. Peter's cock leaked precum, and he insistently pressed in a little. It didn't hurt, exactly, but Carson didn't think he'd be able to go to work after three poundings so close together.

"I have to be at work…" he checked his phone. "…in an hour."

"Then we go in shower, then eat," the bear said, giving the back of his neck a kiss. "I can be a little late."

They didn't fuck in the shower again, but the fox was grateful for someone else to help shampoo his fur. As the dryers started up, the bear pulled him into a kiss that nearly made him forget how sore he was. The bear's arms wrapped around him, and only loosened when he needed to turn around to dry his chest.

"I will drive you to work," Peter said.

"I can bike it," he said, even if he wasn't really sure.

"I drive you," the bear insisted.

"Fine," the fox said as he turned the dryers off. As he started to brush out his fur, he remembered something else from yesterday. "Richard and I are going to a club after work. Do you want to come with us?"

"Sure," Peter said, pulling on a tailored gray suit that had been left next to the sink. The fox noticed a clean t-shirt and jeans for him as well. Marshall must have stepped in while they'd been in the shower. Weirdly, now that didn't bother him as much. Seeing somebody's dick really broke a lot of social barriers.

"There's bacon and toast in the kitchen," Marshall called through the door. As the fox left the bathroom and then the bedroom, he saw the elevator door closing.

"Is he embarrassed?" the fox called back into the bedroom. He picked up a plate of buttered toast and crisp bacon and started to eat. The butter tasted weird. Maybe it was margarine. His mom had always used the real stuff.

"I think he wants to clean up in his own apartment," Peter said.

"He made us breakfast," Carson replied.

"That is his job," the bear said between bites. "He will do it, no matter what is happening here."

"Oh," was all the fox could say. He finished eating and set the cleared plate in the sink. It felt odd not to be doing his own dishes.

"We need to drive. There will be traffic," Peter said.

"Alright," the fox said, flicking his tail.

Carson didn't know much about cars, since he'd only ever had one in college, but Peter definitely did. When they walked through the parking garage, the fox noticed the silver car that the bear had hit him with, but they walked right past that one to a canary-yellow sports car parked a few spots down. The fox wondered if every car in this line was Peter's, but he didn't have a chance to ask as the doors lifted up.

"Wow..." the fox whispered. If the other car had been classy, this was Heaven. He practically sunk into the chair as he watched the bear heave himself into the driver's seat. It was a stick shift. Now Carson knew he'd never drive it, even if something in his bones said he wanted to dodge traffic while shooting at bad guys, one paw on the wheel.

"I pick you up for the club tonight in this too," the bear said as the engine revved up. The seats practically vibrated.

"There's no back seat," the fox said. "Where'd Richard sit?"

"Right," Peter said as he backed out of the parking space. He took a turn, and they were out in the stormy morning. At least it would rain while Carson was inside.

"The Bentley has room," the bear continued as they eased into traffic. The fox knew that was a pricey car from rap songs, and when he just flicked his ears, Peter continued. "The silver car I knocked you over with."

"You hit me with a car that expensive?" Carson asked. He pulled his tail into his lap. Holy shit. He was very glad they'd hooked up, but the idea of owning cars that probably cost more than his apartment building hurt the fox's brain.

"This is Lamborghini," Peter said. "I have this, Bentley, the limo Marshall drives, and Mercury."

"I know the last one," the fox said. His knowledge of cars was fading fast, so he grasped where he could.

"It is the one from *Rebel Without A Cause*," the bear explained. "I buy it on auction. Very nice car."

"Like, the actual one from the movie?" Why wasn't it in a museum display or something?

"No. Same model. 1949," the bear said. So even his more reasonable-sounding car was actually a classic. The fox was also out of car trivia, so he instead leaned over, nuzzling the bear's arm. The muscles in his arm tensed each time he shifted gear. Carson could practically feel the car wanting to race down the road, jumping ramps. They turned again, and the fox saw the bookstore. Peter expertly glided the car against the curb, causing people on the street to stare. The bear shifted into park and then put an arm around Carson's shoulders, pulling him closer for a kiss on the lips.

"So, a night on the town as boyfriends?" he asked after pulling back.

"Yeah," the fox said. A month ago, it would have never occurred to him to be with only one person for even a week, let alone longer. Now, everything looked a bit different.

Carson climbed out of the car, smirking at some of the pedestrians who eyed him. He wasn't a kept fox by any means, but it definitely felt good right now, even if he only wore a t-shirt. Would it be like this every day? He felt his phone vibrate, but he ignored it right now. Knotz was probably still open from last night.

99

"The spare keys are in my desk," Terrence said as the fox walked by, not looking up. The lion was always on top of things. Was that due to being in a relationship, or did it just come naturally?

Carson would definitely have a lot of time now if he wasn't going to be searching his phone for cock. Dozens of apps would still provide free porn, but he generally didn't surf cock pictures at work anyway, and if he was at home, he had a laptop. Was there a point in keeping Knotz on his phone? He retrieved the lanyard, pulled it over his head, and walked back out into the main store. A dozen or so customers loitered around, only one of which looked ready to buy anything. Today would be a good day, either way. Richard might meet someone nice tonight, while he and Peter would grind on the dance floor.

Work went by quickly, and since Richard didn't come in today, Carson couldn't run any plans by him. *Honeypot* didn't have a cover, but the drinks were pretty pricey. When he thought about it, he realized Peter would probably just pick up the tab, but he preferred to not rely on that. Of course, the coyote was cute, so odds were he wouldn't be paying for his own drinks.

Is this what couples did? Just go out, do something fun, and then go home with no guarantee of fucking? The last time he'd gone to a club had been because there wasn't a top wolf on Knotz that night and he wanted to be tied. Then again, he knew full well sex with Peter would be great. Why would he want to gamble now?

Strange feelings about work aside, the fox realized at lunch he'd left his bike at Peter's. He had some cash for a cab, but a second thought entered his mind. Wasn't this part of being in a relationship?

*Can Marshall bring my bike to Bookkeepers?* He texted Peter.

*Here is his number.* Came the reply. He added the terrier's number to his contacts, then sent a similar message to the butler.

*No problem at all.* Marshall sent. *I will be there in about twenty-five minutes.* That seemed like a very specific number, but he wasn't about to correct a proper English dog. A few angry thoughts about Pratt flared back up, but he suppressed them. The author had been a lesson learned, and he'd gotten a boyfriend out of it. The black fox could just keep doing what he was doing for all Carson cared.

While he helped a customer a few minutes later, Terrence got the fox's attention and pointed at the front doors. The limo was parked outside by the curb, with Marshall standing on the sidewalk, one arm bracing the fox's bike across the back of his shoulders. He was a lot stronger than Carson had thought. He walked outside, smiling at the butler and taking the large bike in both paws.

"Sorry about running off this morning," the dog muttered. "I had not…expected last night."

"Neither did I," the fox said, giving the dog a quick hug around the shoulders. "Don't worry about it."

"I will assume that won't happen again," Marshall said, all his normal composure back.

Carson smiled. "I doubt it. I think me and Peter will be fine with just us."

"Alright, then," the terrier said, nodding. "Will you need anything else while I am in Papillon?"

"Nope," the fox said. "Thanks for running out here."

Marshall looked like he was about to say something. The dog's pointed ears flicked this way and that before he cleared his throat.

"I hope you and Mr. Belov…do well," he finally said.

"Thanks," and Carson gave the bull terrier a kiss on the cheek. It was very easy to see a blush under white fur.

"I have to get back to work," he said. "I'll probably see you later in the week."

"Yes," the bull terrier said before walking back around the car to the driver's door. Carson walked his bike to the back of the store and set it in the back room. The chain was wrapped around the handlebars, but the lock had been cut. He had a replacement at the apartment, and it could wait until then. He couldn't fault Marshall for being thorough.


After a shower, the fox decided on a mesh shirt and tight leather pants. His mom had given them to him when he'd moved back to Papillon, since 'every gay fox should have a pair.' Richard arrived while he was frying some bacon, so he pulled another few slices out of the fridge. They ate a few BLTs before the intercom buzzed again, and then they walked downstairs to find Peter driving a silver car. The Bentley, the fox corrected himself. Maybe he could learn to drive it. That's what a relationship was about, right? Learning from each other?

The valet for *Honeypot* needed a few seconds to recover when he saw the car, and Peter whispered something in his ear while passing him a twenty-dollar bill. Now that they were out in front of the club, the fox noticed the bear had dressed up, in a way; he'd gone with a tight shirt to show off his muscles and a loose pair of pants, both probably more expensive each than the fox's whole wardrobe. He probably owned a dozen suits, but it was nice that he had made the effort.

"I think you're supposed to tip him after we get out," the fox said, and the bear wrapped an arm around his shoulders, kissing one of his ears.

"It is insurance to get it back fine," Peter said. Richard seemed embarrassed by that too, but he didn't say anything.

*Honeypot* had three floors. Most of the first floor was dominated by a dance floor, all strobe lights and foam. Carson could see hundreds of half-naked guys—or maybe entirely naked under the foam—grinding against whomever was closest. The second floor was three different lounges, each with a different aesthetic and all with really hot bartenders. The rumor was they were all straight, so no one could flirt free drinks out of them. The top floor was a pride shop and a VIP longue, split depending on which staircase you took up.

Carson waded into the foam, one paw gripping Peter's and watching as Richard followed them. The fox bet he was embarrassed, but the music was thumping and Carson wanted to enjoy it with his new boyfriend. He started swaying to the beat, pulling Peter against him. The foam came up past his waist, and that meant the bear could sneak a grope if he wanted to, or the other way around. Carson looked up at Peter as they got into sync—the bear couldn't really dance, but he matched the fox's movements.

The fox watched as Richard smiled at a big wolf, who smiled back and waded through the foam to dance next to him. The music was loud, but Carson knew what was happening as the wolf inclined his muzzle to whisper something in his ear. The coyote might not be looking for a random cock, but if someone had said he was cute and offered to buy him a drink, he'd take it too. The two waited for a lull in the music, when people calmed down a little, before walking out of the foam. Carson stood up on his toes and gave the bear a kiss on the lips.

"It very loud in here," he said. "I expected pianos."

"That's *Sera to Steve* on 18th," the fox said before the music picked up again. Almost everything was a dance remix of some popular song, but he didn't mind. He was surrounded by hot guys grinding against one another, and the bear's paws kept sliding between his hips and ass.

They stayed on the floor for a few more songs before stepping out of the foam. It was mostly air, since by the time they made it upstairs their clothes were dry. A few couples were situated on couches, getting in some pre-hookup making out before leaving, since the second people whipped out hard cocks the club kicked them out. A few people walked around wearing nothing but jewelry. Carson walked up to the closest bar.

"Can I get a Long Island Iced Tea?" he asked. The bartender, a fennec who only wore a well-placed fig leaf, nodded without looking up.

"I will have rum and coke," the bear said, leaning on the bar next to him. He smiled at Peter before taking a look around the room.

There was Richard, sitting in a booth next to that wolf, chatting over pink drinks with slices of pineapple in them. Dozens of other hot guys lined the room, some in couples, some in groups, but all there for his visual enjoyment. However, he didn't feel this sheath tingle or his mind wander to what some of them might feel like on top of or under him. He had Peter. Peter was nice. Peter was fun, and when the bear leaned over to kiss him on the cheek, passing the drink into his paw, he remembered to do something.

Carson reached into his pocket with his empty paw and unlocked his phone. He had a dozen messages, and he patiently deleted all of them. With a few swipes he found the actual icon for Knotz, and opened the settings to find the 'delete all content' button.

*Are You Sure?* Read the display. He wasn't sure if this would work out. He wasn't sure if he'd be with Peter for a few months, or for the rest of his life. What he was sure of was that he wanted to try being in a relationship, and if he and the bear went their separate ways, he would try another.

He pressed 'Yes.'

# About the Author

Andres Cyanni Halden writes fantasy, romance, and contemporary fiction, all of which involve talking animals in some way. He has finished a fantasy trilogy, and his short stories have appeared in several anthologies, including *The Fortune Teller's Poem* and *Holidays*. You can probably spot him lurking around tables at conventions, signing any book handed to him. All of his published work can be purchased through *www.FurPlanet.com*.